CAPTURED,

ESCAPE,

REPEAT

A SLEUTH SISTERS MYSTERY

BY

MAGGIE PILL

Gwendolyn Press, Michigan

Captured, Escape, Repeat— Maggie Pill—1st ed.

ISBN: 978-1-944502-25-6

Dedication

For Warren Hauer, who was a great guy and a real character.

CHAPTER ONE

Barb

Faye was at church, probably starting the second hymn, when Retta called me. Our youngest sister, who is often excitable, had progressed to semi-hysterical. "He's gone, Barbara Ann! They say he left, but that's ridiculous!"

"Who's gone, Retta?"

"Lars! He—we—everything was fine—well, he was a little weird, but I thought that was because he was nervous about asking me—and then he just disappeared!"

I tried to imagine a Viking-sized man suddenly dematerializing. "Back up a little. Where are you?"

She sniffed, and I realized she'd been crying. "Green Bay, Wisconsin."

That was the first thing my sister had said that made sense to me. Her boyfriend Lars had come to Michigan to celebrate Christmas with Faye and Dale, Rory and me, and Retta. After the festivities, he and Retta packed both their vehicles with her belongings and started for his home in Albuquerque, New Mexico. What Retta considered essential had filled Lars' pickup, her SUV, and a car-top carrier. Of course, her Newfoundland, Styx, accounted for a large share of the available space. I'd wondered how all of it would fit in Lars' condo, but that wasn't my problem to solve.

They'd left Allport on Friday. The plan had been to go through Michigan's Upper Peninsula, see some sights along the way, and then head south through Wisconsin, so Lars could visit the town where he was born. Lars hadn't seen Peshtigo since he was three years old, so Retta thought of it as a sentimental journey for him. Lars was fifty years old. He could have visited the town of his birth a dozen times if he'd wanted to, but Retta assumes she knows what everyone needs to do to be happy, and because she's so darned cute, she usually gets her way. Especially with Lars.

"It's storming here, and they said it's worse to the south," she was saying. "We stopped early yesterday, figuring we'd head out this morning after the plows cleared the roads." Her voice rose a few tones. "Where is Lars, Barbara Ann?"

"Where were you when he went missing?"

"I was here. He said he had to go out, so I stayed with Styx."

"When you say 'here,' do you mean a motel in Green Bay?"

"Finding one wasn't easy. There's some winter festival going on this week, plus the Packers play at home this afternoon. All the hotels are full, but finally someone sent us to this mom-and-pop place. It's clean, but not exactly fancy."

"So you found a room. Then what happened?"

"I told you! Lars left. He said he'd be right back, but he wasn't. Then I got this awful text and—" She ended with a strangled sob. "Barbara, no one believes me. The Sleuth Sisters need to find Lars!"

We are not the Sleuth Sisters. My sisters and I run a small investigative firm called the Smart Detective Agency. Retta invented a "better" name, which I ignore. Along with preferring her own name for our firm, Retta has her own methods of operating, which often makes her a thorn in my side. Still, Retta has contacts all over the state. She's tougher than she appears and unbelievably courageous when facing trouble. Her downside is that she's also all action and no caution.

"What happened that might explain Lars leaving you alone at the motel?"

"Nothing! Neither of us has ever been to Green Bay before, so we drove around for a while. We found this little strip mall that was really interesting. It wasn't the usual dollar store, pizza place, hair salon, and cash advance joint."

"And Lars was behaving normally?"

"Like I said, he got a little weird while we were in this one shop. We were looking at jewelry, and he saw something that made him act—I don't know, distracted."

"Do you know what it was?"

Her voice changed. "It was this really unusual antique ring. It was beautiful, and I thought..." She paused, and I filled in the rest.

"You thought he was going to ask you to marry him."

"Which is proof Lars didn't dump me in Green Bay, Wisconsin!"

"Dump you?"

"That's what the text said." She repeated the message in a manly tone. *"I've met an old girlfriend and we're going to try again for happiness. I don't want to hear from you again. Goodbye, my dear."* Her voice rose an octave. "I don't believe it for one minute!"

I was as shocked as she was. "Lars broke up with you?"

Retta's voice rose. "No, Barbara Ann, he didn't! In the first place, Lars loves me. Second, he isn't the kind of jerk who'd end a relationship by text. And third, every word is written out in full and spelled correctly. With punctuation. Lars did not send that message."

Having received a couple of texts from Lars, I had to agree on the last point. His "CU L8R" form of communication simply didn't jibe with complete sentences and an old-fashioned, fond farewell. Retta was prone to jumping to conclusions, but this time, I had to agree. Lars was in some kind of trouble.

CHAPTER TWO

Faye

The Sunday service was a restful break from the cares of everyday life, as church is meant to be. Dale's mother Harriet died in her sleep on New Year's Day, 2019. We'd gotten through the visitation, funeral, and dinner with no overt animosity, but our meeting with Harriet's lawyer on Friday had turned Dale's siblings into grumpy crybabies. By Sunday, I needed quiet time and a few hymns about Christian love.

According to her will, the farmhouse where Harriet had raised her family was to be sold, to the current renters if they could manage the low end of its current market value. Money from the sale would be used to pay Harriet's debts, which were blessedly few. Any remaining amount would go to her church for mission work. Each of Harriet's children got his or her choice of one item from the furniture stored in a barn on the property. My husband was the only one content with Harriet's final choices. He asked for a bent-wood rocking chair his grandfather had made in the 1800s. Not to sell, to keep as an heirloom.

The others had grumbled as they pored over the piles of old furniture and appliances, trying to find something that might bring a few bucks on Allport Buy/Sell/Trade. "We should all get a share of the money from selling the farm," Dale's sister Wanda whined. "Gary was hoping there'd be enough for a down payment on a new truck."

With his back to her, Dale rolled his eyes at me. The church had done more for Harriet in the last decade than her four younger children put together. That sounded mean, even inside my head, so it was fitting that the preacher had chosen a sermon based on the thirteenth chapter of First Corinthians: "Love Is Patient and Kind." Except for Dale, Harriet's children had abandoned her in her old age. We'd done her paperwork and run interference when Harriet got nasty with the nursing home staff. I'd never minded (Well, there had been days when I did, just a little) and we didn't expect a reward. Harriet's decision to leave everything to the poor was fine in my book. Dale's four sisters were acting like greedy grinches.

Darn! I'd reverted to unchristian thoughts. Closing my eyes, I tried to generate sympathy for my in-laws. They all needed financial help, but after years of scrabbling for a living, Dale and I were finally okay. We felt lucky. They felt cheated. I forced my mind back to the message. *The greatest of these is love.*

After church I drove home, and entered Barb's rambling house through the rear entrance. Two large rooms at the front served as headquarters for the Smart Detective Agency, and our clients used that entrance. Dale and I and Buddy the dog occupied three cozy rooms in the middle, and the large, country kitchen at the back was shared space.

Barb had made the whole second floor into her apartment, where she retreated in the evenings and worked on whatever kind of puzzle she was into at the time, dined on take-out food, and read with her half-wild cat, Brat, curled up on her lap. I always let her know she was welcome to eat with us, any meal, any time, but she said my cooking was too good and she ate too much. I'm not sure why someone in her fifties still worries about her figure, but Barb is determined her waist size will never match her hips.

The old house was home to Dale and me, and Barb made sure we never felt like interlopers. We helped with expenses, did our part to keep the place up, and lived in our own space, allowing Barb companionship on her terms. She's a solitary sort, which our younger sister Retta has never understood, perhaps because solitude was forced on her when her cop husband was killed. Living in a nice home a few miles outside

Allport, Retta is by far the most social of the three of us, joining a ton of civic, church, and other groups to fill her idle hours.

For decades Barb had lived on the West Coast, but after she retired and came home to Allport, we started a detective agency, intending a two-woman partnership. Baby Sister Retta had wormed her way into our affairs, as she'd done all our lives. I didn't mind, since we each brought something valuable to the job. Barb is an excellent analyst, and people respect her businesslike attitude. Retta isn't shy, and she can easily charm cooperation and information from people. I'm pretty good with a computer, and I like to think I have a knack for sensing people's emotional state: what they need or want at a given moment in time.

Then, just a month ago, Retta had announced a trial move to New Mexico with Lars Johannsen. I tried to be understanding, knowing she needed her chance for happiness, but honestly, doesn't anybody stay in one place anymore?

As I came into the kitchen I could smell the banana-cranberry bread I'd made earlier. Hearing me toeing off my boots, Dale came out of the den. "How was church?"

"Good. You ready to taste my latest concoction?" I filled his coffee cup with the last of the pot's contents and put it in the microwave along with some water for my tea. Sitting down at the table, Dale opened his weather app and began telling me the weather as if I hadn't just been outside in it. I made interested noises as I sugared his coffee, dunked my teabag, and sliced the quick bread, still slightly warm in the middle.

A falling tree branch had left my forester husband with a traumatic brain injury, and though he'd recovered better than the doctors predicted, Dale was most comfortable in quiet spaces with dim lighting. His changed lifestyle had brought on a deep interest in the weather, and he felt almost compelled to report it to everyone he spoke to. We'd all

13

learned to make appropriate noises and act as if we couldn't have found out for ourselves that it was snowing in January in Michigan.

"Big one coming." I set a slice of the quick bread on a napkin for each of us, medium-sized since lunch was less than an hour away. "Dumped a bunch of snow on Wisconsin, and it's gonna pick up moisture again over Lake Michigan."

"Um." Dunking my teabag one more time, I squeezed it against a spoon. Steps sounded in the hallway, and I looked up. "Hey, Barb."

"We have a situation."

"Have a snack with us," Dale advised. "Not many situations Faye's baking can't improve."

With uncharacteristic disregard for her calorie count, Barb sat next to Dale and took a slice. I got her a plate and a glass of water then took the chair opposite her. "What's up?"

"Retta's in Green Bay, and she says Lars has disappeared."

Dale and I both reacted to the statement. "What?"

Barb filled us in, and Dale asked, "Did she call the hospitals?"

"She says no one has a Lars Johannsen or a John Doe matching his description."

"How about the police?"

Barb made a disgusted moue. "Apparently they aren't very interested. First there's the text, which they accept at face value. It came from Lars' phone. It gives a reason for his absence. He's not responding to calls, but they suggest it's because he doesn't want to talk to her.

Retta says the cops 'smirked' when she explained why she's sure Lars hasn't dumped her, and they probably did, not knowing her and Lars."

"But we know Lars," I said. "It really doesn't sound like him."

"Maybe she should call his people in Albuquerque," Dale suggested.

"She did. He's officially on vacation for another week, and of course they weren't about to share information with a strange woman on the phone." Barb took a bite and swallowed before adding, "And before you ask, she called the condo in Albuquerque and sweet-talked the manager. All he knows is that Lars said he'd return on Friday."

"What do we do?"

Barb sighed. "I'm going to Green Bay. Even if Lars is shacked up with some woman from his past, I can't fault Retta for wanting him to say to her face that they're finished."

I looked at Dale, who'd just lost his mother. Though the business end of things was mostly under control, someone had to deal with personal items we'd cleared from her room in the nursing home and stacked in corners. Her clothing. Her toiletries. Knick-knacks. There were thank-you notes to send, dishes to return, and a dozen other things that would come up unexpectedly. He'd handled it well so far, but was it fair to leave him alone to face that along with the emotional loss?

"Go," he said firmly. "Buddy and I can handle the home front."

My dog, who was sleeping in the doorway in order to be as much of an obstruction as possible, snuffled in his sleep, which sounded like an affirmation.

"We'll both go," I told Barb.

"I'd better check the forecast." Dale took up his phone. "You girls don't want to run into an unexpected weather event on the way."

Chapter Three

Retta

Though it seemed like days before Barbara and Faye could reach me, it would actually be only eight or nine hours. The storm that held Lars and me up on Saturday had passed on, headed southeast, and in typical Midwest fashion, road crews had dealt with the snow efficiently. All northern counties between Allport and Green Bay reported clear roads.

I spent the day focused on two things: new places to look for Lars and a hotel room for my sisters. I had no luck with either. A second and third call to the local police got me nowhere. Though polite, they became more distant each time, and I imagined them shaking their heads. *Poor woman can't accept that her guy bailed.*

As far as getting rooms for my sisters, people actually laughed at me for asking. "Everybody's sold out all week," the owner of my current motel told me. "During winter festival, people stay all the way up in Shawano and even Marinette."

Thinking of the tiny space I occupied, I sighed. "I guess we'll have to share."

He raised a brow. "Three women in there? That should be fun."

That wasn't exactly the word I'd have chosen. The room was small for two, and there was my dog to consider. So far Styx had been really good about being cooped up, but I knew what Barbara would say about sharing a room with him. Still, I tried to be positive. "We'll manage."

After striking out with the police and the FBI, I realized I shouldn't have been completely honest with them. As soon as I mentioned the text, their level of concern dropped dramatically. The woman I spoke to at the

Albuquerque FBI office asked me to read her the message then took a cool tone. "It's possible Agent Johannsen said exactly what he meant, Ms. Stilson."

"Do you know Lars at all?"

"Not well." Her tone said she'd noticed him, and one would, since he's gorgeous. "But he seems to know what he wants and doesn't want from life."

Men don't just walk away from me, and I wasn't going to let some snotty receptionist suggest otherwise. "I know Lars *very* well, and I'm telling you, something is wrong."

I imagined her wrinkling her nose before she responded. "I've taken down your information, Ms. Stilson. Agent Johannsen's superiors will be informed of your concerns."

Since she was polite, I was too. "Bless your heart."

CHAPTER FOUR

Barb

Highway 2 edges Lake Michigan across most of Michigan's Upper Peninsula before heading onward to the Pacific Ocean. After the heavy snowfall, the roadsides were coated with a bright, new coating of white that sparkled in the crisp sunlight. Everywhere people were digging out, using trucks, snow-throwers, and shovels. On the shoulders snowmobile tracks curved in and out, following the road's direction but refusing to copy its boring straightness.

We left the highway at Escanaba, following the lake shore southwest to Menominee, and picked up Highway 41, which took us to Green Bay, Wisconsin, a pleasant town on the Fox River and—you guessed it—Green Bay. It's mostly known as the home of the Packers, the third-oldest franchise in the NFL. The team has played in their original city longer than any other team in the league, and their fans are a breed apart. The Packers are the only NFL team that is non-profit and owned by the people, and Packer fans flock to games played in their open stadium, Lambeau Field, in temperatures from balmy to (more commonly) frigid. Lucky folks in the front rows celebrate with players who, when they score a touchdown, are almost required to do the "Lambeau Leap," a jump into the stands that gets them pummeled by adoring admirers.

Why call a football team the Packers? I wondered, and when we stopped for a potty break, my phone provided the answer. The team's founder, Curly Lambeau, solicited funds for uniforms from his employer, the Indian Packing Company. He was given $500, which translates to about $7,100 today, for uniforms and equipment on the condition that the team be named for its sponsor.

Though I don't watch much television, I enjoy live sports, often with my significant other, Allport's Chief of Police Rory Neuencamp. Being a retired Chicago cop, Rory's a die-hard Bears fan, and we carried on a friendly rivalry over Bears and Lions, Cubs and Tigers, Bulls and Pistons. Since the Packers get to the playoffs more often than either the Bears or the Lions, we usually ended up following them late in the season in hopes of a Super Bowl appearance for a team from the NFC North. Though I continued to hope for Detroit's resurgence, I admired the Packers' tradition of loyal fans and football excellence.

It's one thing to admire something from a distance. It's quite another to witness Packer Game Day up close and personal. According to the GPS, when we left 41 we were eight minutes from the motel Retta was staying in, a 20-unit enterprise called the Pack Rack. The GPS reckoning didn't take into account that it was game day during the playoffs, and the contest had just ended in a win for the Packers. The streets were jammed with raucous, rowdy fans who'd probably started tail-gating at ten that morning and were now headed home, sort of. Apparently driving around wearing a huge hunk of foam cheese on one's head, honking the horn, and shouting, "We're Number One!" over and over was a precursor to actually pointing the car in the direction of one's residence. Faye and I were stuck, and my only consolation was that my SUV didn't have team logos anywhere on it. It was bad enough that we sported Michigan plates.

After crawling along for twenty minutes, we finally turned onto Broadway, where the GPS recalculated and set us back on course. From there it wasn't far to the Pack Rack Motel, which was about as impressive-looking as one might imagine from its name. The roof was green. The cinder-block exterior was painted yellow. There was a burly football player on the sign, and the rooms each had a name beneath the number on the door. I wouldn't have figured it out except Room 4 had *Favre* routered on a board under the numeral. Most football fans my age know Brett's jersey number. That led to a few other names I recalled, like *Starr* at #15, *Rogers* on #12, *Stenerud* on #10, *Hornung* at #5. Of course, #1 was *Lambeau*. The fact that the place only had twenty rooms limited the heroes to offense in most cases, but it was a cute idea.

"Who would paint a business green and yellow?" Faye asked. My sister has never developed an interest in sports, and she often wonders aloud why people care about a bunch of guys in tights chasing a ball around a hundred yards of turf.

"It's the Packer colors," I explained.

"Huh." Her tone said she still didn't get it.

The place wasn't fancy but appeared to be well-maintained. The parking lot was clear of snow and Retta's Acadia sat before Room #14 (*Hutson*). Our trip was over. Our investigation was about to begin.

Retta had been watching, and she opened the door and waved us into the spot next to hers. "The manager's kind of fussy about parking in your own spot," she told us, "but the people in #13 came on a bus from Ashland. They said you can use theirs."

That was when she confessed there were no rooms available for Faye and me. We'd be sharing Retta's room, which was approximately the size of a cell at the Fox County Jail—not that I knew those dimensions for certain. Next to the door was a rack with four pegs, the extent of hanging storage. At the center was a double bed that would have been torture for poor Lars, who was well over six feet. It would be equally tortuous for three middle-aged women to share.

"Mr. Hauer is bringing in a cot," Retta said apologetically.

I wanted to ask where we'd put it, but what would be the point? The head of the bed rested against an interior wall that enclosed the bathroom.

21

A clunky heater/AC unit filled in what was left of the back wall. Along the fourth wall was a pressed-wood dresser with a TV set on top, a small desk, and an office chair the color of spoiled avocados. The bedspread was green, and the white wall had a stripe of bright yellow at eye level.

Then there was Styx. Closed in the bathroom, the Newfoundland started barking and throwing himself at the door as soon as he heard Faye's voice. I shuddered to think of the damage he might do to the cheap wood laminate attempting to get out to greet her. Styx hasn't got a mean bone, but his size and energy level mean collateral damage wherever he goes.

"I made him a bed in the bathtub," Retta told us. "So far he's been very good, but I'll probably have to find him a kennel tomorrow." She looked my way as if inviting me to disagree. "If you think I should."

"Great idea." I was considering sleeping in my car, but as an over-fifty woman, I needed access to a bathroom at least once each night. I looked again at the lumpy bed. Maybe we could sleep in shifts.

Faye gave Retta a second hug. "We're here to help, Sweetie."

"And I'm so glad." For a moment I thought Retta would break down, and I made a vow to be patient. She'd lost her beloved husband too early. Now she faced the possible loss of her second love.

Pulling herself together, she waved at the stark room. "Have a seat...somewhere."

I hauled the slightly cockeyed desk chair out and sat. Faye piled some pillows against the headboard and made herself a nest on the bed. Retta perched between us, at the foot, as agitated as I've ever seen her.

"I take it you haven't learned anything more." If she had, she'd have texted. Retta is an avid, almost rabid, texter.

"No." Tears welled in her eyes and Faye scooted to her side and slid an arm around her, ready, as always, to comfort and support. Retta leaned against her for a moment, her mouth working, and Faye shot me a worried glance. In an investigation, emotion is a two-edged sword. Engagement with a victim gives a detective incentive, but it can also make her careless, even rash.

"I called everyone I could think of. Nobody knows where Lars is." Retta tried to smile. "I even drove around Green Bay for several hours, hoping to catch a glimpse of his pickup. Nothing."

"With all that's going on, it would be hard to spot an individual vehicle," I said.

"That's true. Traffic was crazy, so it was hard to look down side streets and into parking lots."

"We'll go out together in the morning," Faye told her. "There'll be fewer cars."

"That's good." I knew, as no doubt Faye did, that cruising city streets looking for Lars' truck was a longshot, but it was something Retta could do to keep busy. "While you two do that, I'll retrace your route from the time you arrived in Green Bay until you got that text." Taking out my phone I ordered, "Tell me everything you and Lars did."

This was often the point where Retta presented her own ideas about how we should proceed. A few months back we'd had a case where funds were missing from a church's accounts. The pastor suspected the secretary but hadn't wanted to go to the police, so he'd hired us to look into it discreetly. Retta's idea was to visit the church office in disguise. "I'll get her talking and confess that I'm in debt and don't know which way to turn. Then she'll say something about knowing what that's like, and I'll play it by ear from there."

I'd overruled that in favor of having Faye do some forensic accounting, which she's good at due to decades of office management. Once she'd matched the discrepancies in the church's books with deposits to the secretary's personal checking account, I sat down with the pastor and the woman and laid out our evidence. She'd collapsed in tears, claimed she meant to pay the money back, and begged to be given time. I had left at that point, figuring the rest was up to the pastor. Case closed, no disguise required.

With experiences like that as prologue, I waited for Retta to present her ideas on what we should do. Instead, she simply agreed with my proposal. Once I recovered from my surprise, I began listing the places she described in my memo app.

Gas station: They'd both filled their tanks in preparation for continuing southward Sunday morning. She didn't remember the name of the place but found the receipt in her purse. I copied down the address and the time she'd been there.

Motel: They'd checked in at three p.m. on Saturday after finding that the Pack Rack was the only place in town with a room available.

Shoppers' mall: Before going to dinner they'd stopped at a strip mall that advertised itself as "unique." That was true, Retta claimed, and they'd spent an hour wandering through antiques, collectibles, and craft items. There'd been four stores, possibly five, located in an old mill near the river. Though she didn't recall the address, there was a business across the street called Potter's Plumbing. "The name was funny, and I pointed it out to Lars."

"A store in the antique mall is where he began acting strangely?"

Retta frowned. "He got distracted, like he was thinking about something."

"And you thought it was because of a ring."

She shrugged. "I asked to see a pair of earrings, and I noticed Lars looking at what was next to them in the case. I talked to the woman behind the counter a little. She was wearing a beautiful necklace of jet, and I told her about Mom's triple loop she inherited from Grandma Eames. Lars asked her where they get their stuff, and she said mostly from estates." Retta smiled. "They sell online too, and the lady was really cute. I mean, she was seventy-five if she was a day, and she tossed out terms like *ROI* and *SEO* like you wouldn't believe."

"But Lars seemed different after that."

"Distracted, like I said. He asked how late they were open, and the woman said on Saturdays she was there until nine."

"You think he intended to go back there?"

"I thought so, but the mall is closed on Sundays, so I haven't been able to ask."

"You and Faye can do that in the morning." I wrote *Antique store.* "What's next?"

"Dinner." I wrote down *Restaurant.* "We were going to go to Brett Favre's Steakhouse, but it's now the Hall of Fame Chophouse, which Lars didn't find nearly as interesting. Besides that, the parking lot was packed. We ended up at a place called the Green Bistro, nice but a little pricey. I brought home part of my dinner for Styx." She smiled at the dog, who sat with his big head on Faye's lap. If she stopped petting him he gave her a nudge to let her know he wasn't ready for her to be done.

"Did anything unusual happen at the bistro?"

"No, though we had to wait a while for our food. Like everywhere else in town, it was packed." Retta's sense of humor peeped through as she added, "No pun intended."

"Then you came back here?"

She thought about that. "We stopped and got a bottle of Crown Royal. In Wisconsin, liquor's only sold at state-run stores. Lars joked we should stock up, because if the storm got worse, we'd have nothing to do but drink and…" She blushed, adding, "You know."

I wrote down *Liquor store*. "Okay, when you got back here, Lars said he had to go out again."

"Right. He borrowed my tablet to look at something then told me he had to go out for a half hour or so for work. He seemed secretive, and I thought of that ring and figured he meant to go buy it."

"Okay," I told them, setting my list aside, "in the morning, you two cruise the streets then visit the strip mall and talk to the people there. They'll open by ten, I would think."

Retta's eyes again filled with tears. "Do I have to tell you girls how wonderful you are to come here and help me? I know we'll find out what's keeping Lars away."

There was no sense saying aloud that despite the odd wording of the text, Lars might have done exactly what it said. He might have met an old flame. He might have had second thoughts about Retta and Styx moving in with him. Styx wasn't like having a dog around; he was like having six dogs. And if Retta made a fuss about the ring they'd seen, Lars might have concluded she expected a proposal. While he'd never said much about his first marriage, I knew its ending hadn't been peaceful. What if he'd felt pressured and didn't want to take that plunge again?

That reminded me of something. "Did you call Lars' kids?"

Retta's lips twisted. "They both acted like I'm stalking their father, but they did say they hadn't heard from him since before we left Allport."

A knock on the door interrupted us, and Retta went to open it. "Here's your cot!" A very tall man whose rich, bass voice echoed in the tiny room pushed in a rickety-looking frame folded around a ratty-looking mattress. There followed some shifting of furniture and personal items to accommodate the thing. While Retta held Styx back from loving the guy to death, Faye and I helped him push the double bed into the corner.

Retta had gathered Lars' things and put them under the shelf by the door, but the room was still cluttered with her stuff. Wherever Retta went, makeup, toiletries, and accessories appeared like petals strewn by a half-crazed flower girl. Luckily Faye and I were pretty much natural types who didn't require vanity space or corners in which to set four extra pairs of shoes. Though I wasn't used to living in the midst of such clutter, I told myself I'd get used to it. Temporarily.

When Hauer had the cot set up, he wished us goodnight and went on his way. We stood for a moment, looking at our sleeping space. "Retta, since you don't get up to pee in the night, you get the inside of the big bed," I said. "I'll take the cot." I'd have paid triple the going rate for a room of my own, and I saw sympathy on Faye's face. No matter how much I love someone, I like my own space to retreat to at the end of the day.

As usual, Retta saw the situation differently. "This is like when we were kids and all slept in your room when it stormed, Barbara Ann." Her expression grew serious as she added, "As scared as I used to get back then, I think I'm more scared right now."

CHAPTER FIVE

Faye

I woke at four, unused to the bed and the absence of Dale beside me. My sisters didn't snore, and I'd grown used to my husband's snuffs and whistles and almost depended on them to help me sleep. Retta didn't drift off for a long time, but when she did, she made little, unconscious mews of anxiety. At five-thirty I finally eased out from the sheets, went to the desk, and opened the solitaire game on my phone. At seven I was reading the news when Barb rolled over, opened her eyes, and gave me a thin smile. "How was your bed?"

"Like the hills of Ireland, soft and rolling."

"This one's like the Rockies, hard and lumpy." She sat up, tossed the blanket aside, and ran a hand through her graying hair. "How's Sleeping Beauty?"

"I'm awake," Retta said, though she didn't turn to face us. "Faye, what's the weather like?"

I'd already checked. "They're predicting sunshine and clear skies, though the temps will be in the low thirties."

"Stay where you are, Retta," Barb ordered. "I'll shower, then Faye, then you."

"Why do I go last?"

"Because you take the longest, but don't get all mad. Tomorrow you can go first."

After we had breakfast at a diner near the motel, Barb left in her Edge to retrace Lars and Retta's route on Saturday, hoping someone had noticed a threat, possibly a person following Lars. As an FBI agent, he had enemies in the criminal world. If someone he'd once arrested noticed him driving around Green Bay…I really didn't know where that notion led, but Barb said it should be checked out.

While she did that, Retta and I took Styx to a boarding kennel. He hadn't settled in well during the night, and Retta had crept over me several times to speak to him as sternly as I've ever heard her. It did no good. The dog knew things were upset, and while he didn't get why, he was agitated. Barb never mentioned the whining and constant movement in the bathroom, but her expression was easy to read. Another night with a Newf in our space was out of the question.

We visited three boarding kennels before Retta found one where she'd actually leave her dog. The first two were much too restrictive for Styx, who's got more energy than most nuclear power plants. The third had plenty of room to run, and the people seemed pleased to have him. Retta was sad to leave Styx there nonetheless, and I understood, since I was already missing my own little bundle of orneriness. Leaving your fur baby with strangers is always difficult, and Retta already had plenty of stress. Still, we had to focus on finding Lars, and with Styx in our tiny motel room, there was no such thing as focus.

When we got him settled in, it wasn't yet ten o'clock. To fill the time until the little mall opened, I drove around Green Bay while Retta peered out the front and side windows, looking for Lars' vehicle. We located a few dark green Denali trucks, but when we got close enough to investigate, none had New Mexico plates.

At ten fifteen we pulled into the parking lot of the antique mall, which was situated on a corner with busy streets at its front and west sides. A sign proclaimed *The Old Mill,* and Retta explained that flour had once been manufactured there. The building was slightly decrepit but charming, and the location offered the shop owners good visibility from the road. Behind the mill was a junkyard fenced with galvanized panels, so while the view wasn't exactly picturesque, it was neat.

The mill itself was three stories high on one end and two the rest of the way, with a gambrel roof and a wide, raised platform in front that had once been a loading dock. Along it were five entry points, and a sign over each boasted some sort of specialty shop. Critterz, the largest, was situated at the three-story end of the building. A covered outdoor staircase, no doubt a fire exit, zig-zagged down the exterior wall.

I surveyed the four smaller shops' offerings: books, CDs, and records in one; dolls and toys in another; sports memorabilia in a third; and handmade fabric crafts in the last. Critterz had, according to a sign, *Everything for the Collector and Some Things You Never Imagined.*

We climbed a wide staircase at the center to reach the platform, but I was pleased to see a ramp on the east end. Having lived with a disabled person, I'd seen too many businesses with stairs to navigate, narrow passageways, or doors that open the wrong way. Though Dale's ability to get around had improved over time, it still upset me when I saw accessibility laws ignored.

Critterz had a small army of cats prancing and playing on its sign. The first thing I saw as I closed the door behind us was a live version, a calico tabby with a blue collar who faced us like a sentry, his resting place an ornate telephone desk. He stayed put, but two other cats crouched and ran at the sight of us. In one case all I saw was a tail disappearing under an old dry sink.

The room we entered was chilly, and I guessed it was problematic to heat a space so large. Above us, old pipes ran along the ceiling in every direction, some small, some large enough for a cat to climb through. This was proven when a gray tabby poked its head out from an open end, glared at us for a moment, and retreated.

"Interesting, isn't it?" Retta asked. "They left what they could of the old mill in place, so it's part store, part museum."

In front of me was an eight-inch-square post, one of several scattered around the room, with a small, wooden trapdoor at chest level. Opening the cover, I saw that the pillars were actually chutes where flour of different types would once have tumbled from the grinding machinery on the level above down to this floor. I imagined men waiting with grain sacks, holding them under the chute as they filled then hauling the sacks to the loading dock for transport.

I paused for a moment, taking in the sight of...stuff. Pathways wove right and left, and goods of all kinds lined the aisles, both ways. I can't begin to list everything, but the word *eclectic* came to mind. There were delicate figurines, collectible dishes of a dozen different kinds, chairs, cabinets, bed frames, vintage clothing, oddities from other eras, and more. And more. Special displays in the corners recreated old-fashioned scenes: a kitchen with vintage gadgets, a child's bedroom dotted with antique toys, and a Victorian man-cave with pipes and heavy furniture. As we wove our way through, I was unable to keep from pointing things out.

"Look!" I pointed. "Didn't Mom have a punch bowl like that?"

"I borrowed it once for a Barbie Party," Retta confessed. "Afterward she had eight of those little hooks that hang over the rim but only seven cups to hang on them."

Next I gestured at a lumpy shape on a table near the wall. "Is that a Xerox machine under that cover? I remember the teachers making

31

worksheets for us on those. They'd crank that thing and paper would shoot out with that clunkety-clunk sound."

"Yeah," Retta responded. "By spring, every single quiz had a blurry spot down the middle."

Remembering our purpose, we moved on. At the back of the store was a long, glass-front counter that was itself an antique. Inside it was jewelry, and behind it a very tall woman was taking money from a tin box and sorting it into the compartments of an antique cash register. At one end a pot-bellied stove pumped out heat, and behind it I saw a half-full wood-box.

"That's not the woman who was working on Saturday." Retta's voice revealed disappointment. "And the ring is gone."

"Hello, there." The woman looked to be in her early eighties, with baggy eyes and a droopy mouth. Some tall people adapt to a world too low for comfort by stooping, and she was one of those. The permanent bend in her back caused her to stretch her neck forward and turn her head up, giving her the unfortunate silhouette of a condor. She had a mellow, pleasant voice and the manner of an old-time librarian. Her outfit, a plain white blouse, black slacks, and a necklace hung with tiny plastic beads in green and yellow, fit right into the stereotype. She even had a pair of half-glasses set low on her nose and fastened to a beaded chain that kept them around her neck. The only non-librarian touch was her watch, which had a yellow football helmet with a green *G* for its face and little footballs at the end of the hour and minute hands. "Can I help you?"

Retta stepped forward. "On Saturday there was a different woman working."

"My sister DeeAnne. Is there a problem?"

32

"No. It's just that I was hoping to speak with her about something that happened that night." Retta bit her lip. "It's kind of important."

Our hostess thought about it for a second. "I can call and see if she's willing to come down."

Retta brightened. "She's upstairs?"

"We live up there." She pointed. "We own the whole building, and there's plenty of space in the half-story for us and our kitty-cats."

"Two sisters who live together," Retta said. "How nice."

"Actually there are three of us. I'm Betty White." She rolled her eyes. "And I've already heard it, so don't say a word. My sister DeeAnne, whom you already met, minds the store with me, and our sister Lydia does the bookkeeping and such."

"A family business!" Retta glanced at me.

"We like it. Excuse me for a moment, and I'll see if Dee's busy." Turning away, she spoke into a phone briefly, set it back in her pocket, and told us, "She'll be right down." Waggling a finger she added, "I should warn you that when my sister says 'right down,' it could be anything from three minutes to thirty."

That sounded like Retta, but of course I didn't say it aloud. Instead I began the polite conversation waiting requires. "Gathering all this inventory must take a lot of work."

Betty nodded. "When I started the business years ago, I'd drive all over the state scouring garage sales and auctions for merchandise I could turn a profit on." She gestured to where a cane leaned on the wall behind her. "Ten years ago—no, it was closer to eleven, because that was the year we had so much snow. I did my own shoveling then, the whole front

33

porch and the steps. Bob Waverly did the parking lot with his plow truck, but I did all the rest. I could barely keep up that year, there was so much snow." Remembering she'd started in a different direction, she stopped. "Anyway. I had a bad fall, and the doctors did the best they could with my hip, but there was arthritis and some osteoporosis too. Without my sisters, I don't know what I'd have done."

"Sisters are the best," Retta murmured. "Is your hip better now?"

"It holds me up." She raised her brows. "That's all I can ask."

"That's too bad."

Betty flashed obviously false teeth at us. "You know what they say: As long as you're still kicking, things could be worse. I'm just not kicking as high as I used to. Anyhow, our younger sister Lydia handles the business end of things now. She has a real eye for value."

"Younger siblings are often more in tune with how the world works," Retta said pointedly.

"That's true," Betty agreed. "She got us onto the internet, so people don't actually have to come to Wisconsin to find our little treasures." She pointed at the computer. "Even I can search the inventory and tell you if we've got what you want."

"Who transports your merchandise?" I asked. "That's hard work."

"My grand-niece and nephew do the traveling and heavy lifting." Betty's tone turned slightly embarrassed as she confided, "Lydia watches the obituaries then contacts the heirs and offers a flat price for the estate."

"There's a lot of that in Florida." Retta said. "Kids don't want to deal with Mom's stuff, so they hire someone to haul it away."

"My grand-niece sorts through everything for us," Betty said proudly. "We don't deal in badly-crocheted doilies and old VHS tapes."

"It sounds like you have a good system worked out."

"Lydia does. These days I mostly just mind the store and work on my Packerphrenalia collection."

"Your what?"

She smiled slyly. "I collect Green Bay Packer items." Stepping back, she pulled up her pant-legs to reveal green socks with the Packer logo on each ankle. "I've always been a fan, and the second-hand business gave me plenty of opportunity to collect team-related items." Turning, she took a bulky scrapbook from the shelf behind her and set it on the counter. Paging through, she noted the glory years of the team. The Super Bowl wins of 1967 and 1968 were favorites, and she had photos of every member of the '68 team, labeled with their position and their important statistics. In some of the photos she stood beside the player, as tall as the men she admired though only half as wide.

She went on and on, talking about long-dead football players as if they were old friends. I'd heard Packer fans were unique, but this one seemed to be a little extreme, maybe a few sandwiches short of a picnic.

Retta did an admirable job of oohing and aahing as Betty went on and on, reminded at each page of a new reason for loving the team. Some of the names she mentioned struck a chord in my memory, but I soon got tired of listening and wondered when the other sister was coming downstairs.

When a whirr sounded to our left, I turned to see a freight elevator in the corner shudder to life. About four feet square and enclosed in a metal cage, the car, also enclosed with mesh, chugged like a spent runner as it rose. "I use that contraption because of my hip," Betty explained. "Dee just likes to make an entrance."

Seconds later the cage descended again. In it was a tiny woman in her mid-seventies with improbably red hair and liberally applied makeup. She wore an outfit that belonged on the catwalks of Milan: tight leggings in crimson, a drape-y top with wide sleeves, and a bright yellow beret. Nobody spoke for a few seconds due to the jerks, squeals, and grinds of the machinery. When the car stopped, DeeAnne opened the safety gate with a flourish and made an entrance worthy of Ruby Keeler. All that was missing was a company of handsome young men in tuxes waiting to lift her on their shoulders and carry her toward us.

"That's her," Retta whispered.

"Dee, these ladies came to see you," Betty said as Dee tripped toward us. I have to say that while I seldom use that word, it was apt in this instance. A calico tabby emerged from a side aisle and followed, its manner typical of cats: *I'm with her but not really* with *her. We just happen to be going in this direction at the same time.* The cat jumped gracefully onto the counter and began rubbing against items, knocking them over or onto the floor. Betty righted them with no visible sign of irritation.

When she reached us, DeeAnne beamed like Glinda the Good Witch greeting all the little people. "How nice to see you again, dear!"

"Nice to see you too. My name is Margaretta Stilson, and this is my sister, Faye Burner."

"Your sister! Isn't that nice!" I reached out to shake hands, and DeeAnne took mine in both of hers, more like a royal blessing than a handshake. "I'm DeeAnne March. And you've met Betty."

"We wanted to ask about the man who came here on Saturday with Retta," I said. "He's missing, and we're worried about him."

Her blue eyes widened. "Missing? What do you mean?"

"After we left here," Retta explained, "Lars and I went to dinner. When we got back to our room at the motel, he said he had to go out again. He never returned."

"Oh, my!" DeeAnne put a hand to her chest *à la* Blanche Dubois. "That's terrible!"

Betty frowned. "You had no indication he might not come back?"

Retta glanced at me before answering. We'd decided not to mention the text, since to those who didn't know him, it seemed to account for Lars' absence. "I thought he might have stopped here."

"What for?"

"He liked a ring we saw." She pointed. "It was in there."

Betty glanced at DeeAnne before turning sad eyes on Retta. "You're worried about where your friend has gone."

"Yes," Retta replied. "I've looked everywhere I can think of."

"You mustn't—" Betty started to say, but her sister interrupted.

"Let me think." DeeAnne frowned prettily, Shirley Temple in thoughtful mode. "I remember you two came in here around five." She gave the cat a full stroke, and it arched its back in response. "We chatted a little about jewelry. That's it, I'm afraid."

"I see." She handed DeeAnne a business card. "If you think of anything..."

Betty walked us to the door, and I noticed the beads of her necklace were actually tiny footballs. The chain her glasses hung from had little Packer helmets on each end. "If there's anything else we can do to help," she said, "please don't hesitate to ask. I can't imagine how it must feel, not knowing where your friend has gone."

Her phrasing hinted that wherever Lars was, he'd chosen to go there himself. Sadly, that might be true. She was no doubt more objective than we were, since neither of us wanted to believe Lars would abandon Retta.

Thanking her again, we left the store. The black cat who'd greeted us was in the same place as before. I gave its head a few scratches, which it accepted as its due, closing its eyes in response. "I guess these are the critters the name refers to," Retta said. "They probably keep the mice out, but I'd get a dog. Three old women living by themselves need more protection than a half-dozen mousers."

In the parking lot, an older woman with her back to us was picking up trash and stuffing it into a plastic grocery bag. Her identity didn't register with me until Retta rolled her eyes. "Geez!" she said out the side of her mouth. "Our sister, the bag lady."

I had to smile. "Well, she did need a new hobby."

Until recently, Barb had sneaked out in the dead of night to correct grammatical errors on signs in public places. After a close call that almost exposed her identity, she'd retired from the role of Allport's Grammar Nazi, which relieved our fears of embarrassment and possible misdemeanor charges. But Barb, a former assistant district attorney, needed to right the wrongs she encountered. While picking up a piece of litter here and there was something she'd often done, lately she'd launched a one-woman crusade to beautify America. Several times Retta and I had been left waiting while Barb retrieved a water bottle or cigarette butt someone had left behind and then hunted up a place to dispose of, or better yet, recycle it. I considered her cause noble, but it wasn't something I could really get excited about. It definitely slowed us down.

Retta found it embarrassing, and she clucked to me about the lack of dignity inherent in policing parking lots and public spaces without group support or official sanction. Sometimes she made remarks in Barb's presence that hinted how pitiful such individual efforts were. So far Barb hadn't responded. I dreaded the day when she did, since my role in that battle would be referee.

Carrying what she'd gathered to a bin at the corner of the building, Barb disposed of it before joining us. "What did you find out?" Without commenting on the garbage thing, Retta reported that the owners of Critterz were unable to help. Barb hadn't learned anything worthwhile at her various stops either. "The gas station attendant didn't even notice you and Lars filling your vehicles, and the liquor store clerk vaguely recalls the 'cute lady and the big guy' but nothing unusual around you. Lars didn't return to either place later."

"So what do we do now?"

"I don't know." Barb's gaze swept the parking lot, and she stopped as she saw something she'd missed earlier. At the bottom of the exterior staircase, someone had held a mini-party, indicated by the presence of three beer bottles set side by side in the snow. "Be right back." Hurrying down the steps, she headed toward the offending empties.

"Barbara Ann!" Retta hissed, but she paid no attention. Climbing the first few steps, Barb picked up the bottles, pressing them against her coat with one arm while she grasped the railing with the other to come back down the snow-covered steps. As she reached ground level, a bit of paper wafted by on the breeze, and she grabbed that as well, stuffing it into her coat pocket before starting back. Retta looked away, lips pursed, while Barb deposited the bottles in a blue recycle can next to the trash bin.

When she rejoined us, Retta brushed at the front of Barb's black pea coat with a gloved hand. "Do you have to play Woodsy Owl everywhere we go? You're probably crawling with germs."

"I find litter to be consistently and unceasingly annoying," Barb said in reply. Remembering the piece of paper she'd picked up, she fished it from her pocket and started back toward the trash bin. Just before she dropped it in, she stopped and pulled the paper close, squinting at it in the bright sunlight. "The Green Bistro. Isn't that where you said you and Lars had dinner, Retta?"

"Yes. What have you got there?"

"A receipt. Dinner for two, Saturday, 5:43."

"Let me see that." Retta took the paper and scanned it. "Ribs, one whole slab, one half slab. Corona and white wine. And the last four digits of Lars' credit card number. This is our dinner!"

The import of her words hit us, and Barb said, "If Lars didn't come back after dinner, how did the receipt get here?"

"Maybe he went to go to a different store," I suggested.

Retta examined the doorways. "We didn't go into the toy store."

"Okay, let's split up and interview people in the other shops."

Back on the porch a few minutes later, we compared notes. The clerk in the used book store told Barb he didn't work weekends. The man in the sports store said he'd worked on Saturday but didn't remember Retta or Lars. The owner of the fabric crafts shop remembered Retta's face but was sure Lars hadn't come back alone later in the evening.

As we talked, a woman came out of the toy store and walked down to the wheelchair ramp, where a coffee can sat at the bend: an informal smoking area. There was already a man there, leaning on the railing and puffing away, and the two exchanged casual greetings. The woman lit a cigarette, pulling smoke into her lungs like she was drowning. As a former smoker myself, I recognized a possibility we hadn't considered. "Hi," I said, approaching her. "We're private detectives, and I'm wondering if you were working Saturday night."

"Every day the place is open," she replied. "You can't make a living in this business hiring someone else to mind the store." She took a drag. "You're real detectives?"

"Yes. So you need to come out here and smoke pretty often?" Her eyes flashed and I added, "Been there, done that."

She frowned. "You quit?"

"Hardest thing I've ever done." She nodded, and I asked, "Did you see a big guy here around closing time? Blond with wide shoulders?"

She flicked the ash and gave it a couple seconds' thought. "Was he wearing a kinda dorky-looking scarf?"

"I bought him that scarf for Christmas!" Retta and Barb had followed me, and Retta added, "It's Eton Grey cashmere."

The woman's expression said more than words could have about the scarf, but she spoke to me. "He came in around eight-thirty, driving a pickup. Dark blue, maybe green. He sat in the truck for a while, like he was thinking. I noticed because men don't usually shop here on their own." She glanced at Retta. "For sure not men in cashmere scarves."

I spoke quickly to block Retta's possible reply. "Where did he go when he got out?"

"Couldn't tell you. It was cold, so I went back inside. That wind!" She shivered. "Whooh!"

"Was anyone with him?" She shook her head. "Did he seem troubled?"

"I didn't think so." She rose, crushed the cigarette butt, and tossed it into the sand-filled can. "I should get back to work. Good luck with your investigation." She went inside, and the other smoker left too, going down the ramp and disappearing around the back of the building.

"He came back here but didn't go into the antique shop. Why?"

"Something made him change his mind." Retta's gaze searched the parking lot as if asking it what it could have been.

"He got out of the truck," Barb said. "No other way for the receipt to get on the ground."

"Can I see that?" I took it from her, read the printed information, and turned it over. Nothing. "This isn't going to convince the police that the text you got wasn't genuine."

Retta's phone burbled a snatch of some tune I didn't know, and she checked the screen. "Unknown."

"Maybe someone you talked to remembered something."

She answered the call, putting it on speaker, and we heard a man's voice. "Is this the woman that's looking for the guy that took off?"

Her face said she didn't like his phrasing, but Retta said, "Yes."

"I was here Saturday night, and I remember the two of you."

"Did you see the man I was with later that night?" Retta asked.

"No, but I heard him talking on the phone."

Retta frowned. "I don't remember him taking a call."

There was a pause before he said, "You were in the corner looking at something. You probably missed it."

Still frowning, she asked, "What did he say?"

"Something about meeting at the Manitowoc Holiday Inn."

Barb's brows knitted, but Retta nodded to indicate she knew it. "Do you recall anything else?"

"No. I remember Manitowoc because my buddy works at the factory where they make the ice machines."

Thanking him, Retta ended the call. "Manitowoc?" Barb asked.

"A town south of here," Retta replied. "Maybe an hour's drive."

"We could call the Holiday Inn," I suggested.

Barb shook her head. "They won't tell you if he's there. And if—" She paused to reword. "The room might be rented under another name."

Retta shook her head in unconscious denial. "My gut tells me Lars isn't in Manitowoc, but you two should drive down and check."

"What are you going to do?"

"Go back to the motel and make some more calls. Now that the weekend is over, I might be able to reach someone higher up and convince them to take this seriously."

Barb didn't like it, but one pass through the parking lot of the Manitowoc Holiday Inn would tell us everything we needed to know. I checked my watch. "We can be back by three. Promise you won't do anything crazy while we're gone."

"I won't. I just want to be here in case Lars calls."

I glanced at Barb, who shrugged. We had to trust that Retta wouldn't get into too much trouble in the next few hours. When a person is a full-grown adult, you can't just order her around, baby sister or not.

CHAPTER SIX

Retta

When Barbara Ann and Faye left, I did exactly as I'd said. I called the Brown County Sheriff's Department; the Green Bay Police Department; and the local tribal law enforcement agency, the Oneida Police. I got polite responses that went absolutely nowhere. They'd checked the places missing people are commonly found. The Oneida officer had sent Lars' photo to the local casinos. "People lose track of time when they get into gambling mode," he told me. "Your man isn't in any casino now, and nobody remembers him. From your description, he seems like someone who'd be noticed."

Thanking him, I ended the call. Lars was not in a hospital. (Thank goodness.) Not mesmerized by a slot machine. (Fat chance.) The Green Bay police had checked local drinking establishments. I couldn't blame them for that, though there was no way Lars was sitting in a booth in some bar, sloshed beyond knowing what time it was. They'd no doubt ordered patrol officers to look in alleys and abandoned buildings in case he'd been attacked and left…I didn't finish that thought.

I'd promised to be careful, but I simply couldn't sit in the teensy hotel room for the next two-and-a-half hours, waiting for my sisters to return. Lars had left to do something he considered important. The fact that he'd never returned indicated he was the victim of some sort of foul play. But where could I look that hadn't already been covered?

My mind kept going back to the old mill. That was where I'd noticed a change in his behavior. That was where he'd returned after dinner. One of those shops had to have been his destination. I got to thinking that we must have missed something there, and I told myself that asking the right question might dredge up something that would help. I headed back to Barry Street, starting at Critterz.

Betty and DeeAnne were both on duty, and judging from the boxes piled on the counter, they were changing their inventory. As I got closer, I saw that Betty was doing most of the work while DeeAnne held one cat and petted another. She kept up a running conversation—not with her sister, but with the cats, telling them how pretty, clever, and generally wonderful they were. In my experience, a person doesn't have to tell cats that. They're born believing it.

Betty moved clumsily back and forth, due to her hip and because DeeAnne was in the way. She didn't seem irritated, and I guessed Betty was, like Faye, a person who doesn't even notice other people's foibles. When she looked up she frowned, and I saw her struggle to place me. No surprise. It often takes me a few seconds to drag up names these days, and Betty was three decades farther along in the process.

"Margaretta Stilson," I reminded them as I pulled off my gloves and stuffed them into my coat pockets. "We haven't found my friend yet, but we know now that he came back here last night. I wondered if you might have remembered something that could help us."

DeeAnne kissed the cat's head and set it down on the counter. "All I know is what I already told you."

My glance fell on the display case. "It looks like you sold a lot of the stuff that was in there Saturday night."

DeeAnne cleared her throat before replying. "A dealer who handles estate jewelry came in and purchased almost everything we had."

"Have the police been here?"

"Just after you left," Betty said. "We couldn't tell them any more than we told you."

"Something happened here," I insisted. "If you didn't see him—"

"We didn't," Betty said. "You can ask Lydia." DeeAnne shot her a glance and she stepped back, licking her lips.

DeeAnne tilted her head *à la* Ingrid Bergman. "Ms. Silman—"

"Stilson."

"Sorry. Ms. Stilson, we want to help. If you can wait a minute while we get these boxes out of the way, I'll go to the other stores with you and urge the owners to think more carefully about what happened." She tilted her head. "You're a stranger, but we're their landlords."

"That would be very kind."

"All right then." DeeAnne slid the glass door of the case open and took out the only remaining tray of jewelry. "In the meantime, take a look at these. Some of the pieces are quite nice."

As I leaned over items I had little interest in, DeeAnne and Betty took the boxes to a door at the back wall that was propped open, revealing staircases going both up and down. DeeAnne began a conversation in which she did most of the talking while Betty nodded. She seemed reluctant, but DeeAnne was insistent. They made an odd pair, the self-consciously elegant DeeAnne and her Plain Jane sister with her odd collection of Packer accessories.

"I have to take these boxes downstairs, Ms. Sallman," DeeAnne finally said, raising her voice. "With the age of our building, we never leave things near the stairway in case of fire." When I nodded, she turned and disappeared through the doorway. Betty stood by the door, showing

47

her dentures in a smile that was too big, almost gruesome. Suddenly there was a tremendous crash, a scream, and a series of ominous bumps.

"Oh, no!" Betty cried. "She fell!"

Hurrying to the doorway, I stopped next to her and peered down the stairs. Below us the dark seemed to go on forever, but I heard DeeAnne whimpering. "Where's the light?" I asked Betty.

"Bottom of the stairs," she replied. "There's a chain overhead."

"That's not very—" It was useless at this point to chide them for safety violations. Taking out my phone, I used it like a flashlight and descended the steps. Following the sound of DeeAnne's moans, I found her lying on her back in the doorway of a small room, her face crumpled with pain. "Betty! Turn on the light," I urged, hearing her slow steps on the stairs.

"I can't find the chain," she called. "I should have brought a flashlight."

"Here. Use my phone."

As soon as she took it from my hand, the situation changed dramatically. With a grip that was surprisingly strong, DeeAnne grabbed my coat and pulled me backward while Betty pushed. Unable to stop myself, I stumbled through the doorway and kept going until I hit the opposite wall. The breath left my body for a moment and I slumped there, trying to figure out what was happening. Before I could recover, the door slammed shut. I was locked inside, and the darkness was complete.

Pushing myself upright, I hurried to the plank door and began banging on it. When I was too tired to pound anymore, I shouted until my throat was raw. It made no difference to the two not-so-sweet little old ladies who'd locked me in their storeroom. I pictured them going back upstairs and smiling benignly at some customer, extolling the virtues of a fifties-era cap gun or a mission oak dresser with a wonky drawer. The barriers between me and them were sturdy walls, thick floors, and heavy, solid-core doors. I kept making noise anyway.

Even as I made my objections known, part of my mind gave the sisters credit for improvisational skills. Their plot had been devised quickly and executed flawlessly. Barbara, Faye, and I often know what the other is thinking, so we can act without much discussion when circumstances require it. The Whites apparently had the same genetic shorthand. It's a sister thing.

When I finally slumped against the door, exhausted, a funny sound caught my attention, something scratching on the other side. My shoulders hunched as I pictured mice, even rats, as my companions. Smacking the plank wall I said, "Go away!"

Instead of skittering rodent feet, I heard a familiar voice. "Retta?"

"Lars!" I put both hands on the wooden surface as if I could touch him through it.

"I've been trying to get your attention, but you were making so much noise you didn't hear me. Are you okay?"

A quick assessment told me I'd be fine. I couldn't see much, but I felt no obvious open wounds. Damp and cold had begun to seep into my skin. My hands felt gritty. My poor D&G purse, which had been squashed between me and the floor, would probably never be the same. And having handed Betty my phone, I had no way to call for help.

"I'm okay," I told him. "Are you?"

"Fine. Are you alone?"

"Yes. They—" A key turned in a lock, and the door swung open. Framed in the glare of an overhead light bulb was a woman who might have been anywhere from fifty-five to seventy-five. She had DeeAnne's dark hair but Betty's plain face, and she fell between them in height. Her mouth looked as if it didn't know how to form a smile. Behind her a cat with white feet and a Charlie Chaplin moustache lurked, peering curiously around her heels.

"Lydia, I presume."

She didn't bother to answer me. "You and your boyfriend have made a mess out of what was a nice operation."

"*Illegal* operation, right?"

"We move a few things off the grid. The locals have no clue, but when the feds get involved..." Letting that trail off, she reached into her pocket. "Here's your phone. Call every police agency you contacted and tell them your boyfriend is no longer missing."

"No."

"Would you rather he was dead?" Raising the hand that didn't hold a flashlight, she showed me a nasty-looking little snub-nose revolver. When I didn't reply, she went on. "Once you do that, you're going to call your sisters and tell them you found your man. You're leaving the state together." She raised a finger. "No coded messages, and no equivocating. Things are dandy. Tell them to go home, and you'll see them soon." After a pause she added, "If you do as you're told, that might even be the truth."

I made the calls, though I fought back tears when I heard Faye's voice. Everything I said was a lie, but Lydia stood there looking like Inspector Javert guarding Jean Valjean, so I had to make it believable.

Of course Faye and Barbara Ann wouldn't accept what I was forced to say for long, just as I'd known Lars wouldn't break up with me via text message. That didn't calm my nerves, since it meant my sisters would stay on in Wisconsin and end up in as much danger as Lars and I were.

Chapter Seven

Faye

There was no green pickup in the parking lot of the Manitowoc Holiday Inn. After driving all the way around the place, we made a quick plan. I entered through the front door while Barb located a side entrance. Giving her a few seconds, I went to reception and waited for the clerk to notice me.

"Can I help you?"

Channeling Retta, I used a chatty tone. "I hope so. My brother and I were supposed to meet here. He lives in Madison, and I live up in Escanaba, so we figured this was about the middle." I felt the blush that accompanies any lie I tell, but I hoped the clerk would think my face was red from the cold. "I went to the Quality Inn, but they have no reservation for me. I got to thinking, maybe he didn't say the Quality Inn. Maybe he said the *Holiday* Inn. Can you check?"

He was a nice kid, a college student, judging by the textbook he'd been poring over, and he replied diffidently, "Ma'am, I'm not allowed to give out information on guests."

"I know that. But you can say if *I* have a reservation, right?" I leaned an elbow on the counter. "My name is Lois Wilson."

He turned to the computer and brought up the current list of guests. "No Lois Wilson."

"Maybe he made both reservations in his name. Could you check for Larry Flick?"

"Hotel policy, ma'am. I can't tell you who's here. We protect the privacy—" He went on, but I'd already pressed the button on my phone that cued Barb it was time for her part in our little play.

Before the clerk finished his excuses, she came hurrying down the hall. "There's a man lying near the third floor elevator doors. I think he had a stroke or something."

The kid scrambled out from behind the desk, and Barb led him away. As soon as they were out of the lobby I took a quick glance to see if there was a second employee in the back. For once, job cut-backs worked in our favor. The office was empty.

Lars wasn't listed as a guest. Scanning the list, I found three singles rented under a woman's name and memorized the numbers.

By the time Barb and the clerk returned, I was out of sight. She expressed amazement that a man who'd seemed so sick had got up and walked away. After apologizing for scaring the guy, she wished him a nice day and joined me around the corner, near the stairs.

All that was for nothing. None of the single women was a likely match for Lars. One was over seventy. One was a nun on her way to a retreat in Canada. The third wasn't in her room, but a chatty maid guessed her age at twenty-five and mentioned "tons" of tattoos, which made her an unlikely former girlfriend for Lars.

We left by the side door, buffeted by a biting wind as we returned to the car. "That lead went nowhere," Barb said, disappointment evident. "Let's go back and get Retta. We'll find somewhere to have lunch and reconnoiter."

I approved of that, since it was almost one-thirty. Barb is one of those people who can skip a meal without really thinking about it. I, on the other hand, have our father's metabolism, and going without food for any extended period makes me light-headed and grumpy. Still, with Lars missing and Baby Sister worried out of her mind, I hadn't wanted to bring up the subject of food. "Retta will probably be ready to get out of that dinky hotel room for a while."

Except she wasn't in the room. Though the space was still cluttered with her things, Retta's car was gone. "We should have known she'd go off on her own," Barb said disgustedly. "That girl never thinks things through. Whatever comes into her head, she does it!"

"The question is what do *we* do?"

"I guess we wait. We can't report her missing after only a few hours."

The wait wasn't pleasant. Barb paced, as she does when she's agitated. She said unkind things about Retta's brain, and I couldn't argue. Why had she gone off without us? She must have thought whatever she meant to do was safe. I hoped she was right, and the delay was merely Retta being Retta, responding to no timetable but her own.

When my phone rang and I saw her name on the screen, I breathed a sigh of relief. "It's her." Hitting the speaker button I said, "Retta? Where are you?"

"Faye, I'm okay. I found Lars. Everything is fine, and we're going to continue on to Albuquerque. I'll let you know when we get there."

Frowning, I hit the speaker button. "What do you mean?"

"I said we're fine. I called the police and told them Lars is no longer missing." She paused. "Look, I love, love, love you and Barb for coming to my rescue, but you can go home now. We're heading south, so I won't see you for"—Her voice wavered—"for a while."

I looked around. "Your overnight bag is here, and your stuff."

"Take it back to Michigan with you. I'll get it next time I visit."

"Retta—"

"I have to go, Faye." As I opened my mouth to argue she said, "Lars wants to get back on schedule." She hung up.

Barb shook her head in disbelief. "What was that about?"

I shrugged. "No idea."

Packing up Retta's things, I put her suitcase beside Lars' near the exit. That gave us more room, but it was depressing, like the times after Dad and then Mom passed away when we had to decide what to do with their belongings. I told myself it wasn't the same. Retta was *not* dead. She'd call again later and explain everything.

When someone knocked at the door, I opened it to find our host, Warren Hauer. "Hi, ladies. Is Ms. Stilson here?"

"Um, no."

His jaw jutted sideways. "Huh. The kennel where she put her dog just called. There's a problem, and they need to speak with her."

"Wait," Barb said. "Styx is still at the kennel?"

"Yes. They called her first, but she didn't answer her phone. She'd mentioned she was staying here, so they asked me to relay a message."

"What's wrong with Styx?"

Hauer scratched his neck. "I guess he tunneled out and escaped."

I took a step back. "Escaped?"

"They've got people out looking for him, but they thought they'd better let her know."

I opened my mouth to comment but Barb spoke first. "We'll take care of it. And we'll be staying at least one more night."

When he was gone she said, "Take my car. See if they've found Styx."

"Barb, she wouldn't leave him behind."

"I know that."

"But that means—"

"I know what it means," she said in as sharp a tone as she's ever used with me. "We're going to find her. While you look for the dog, I'll call the police and tell them what's happened."

The drive to Pretters' Dog Kennel should have been pleasant. The trees were coldly beautiful, their trunks dark silhouettes and their branches still coated with snow from the storm. The gravel road was clear, with neat, three-foot snowbanks on either side. Sunlight on old cornfields made them look as if they'd been scattered with rhinestones. It was beautiful, but none of it could lift my mood.

The fact that Styx had been left at the kennel meant Retta was not on her way to Albuquerque. Lars had been either killed or kidnapped, and whoever had done that now controlled her. And Styx was out here somewhere, wandering territory strange to him in winter conditions.

I wondered whether I should call Retta's kids and tell them…what? That Aunt Barb and I had somehow lost their mother? We shouldn't have left her alone, but that was hindsight. Retta's always been headstrong and impulsive. She must have thought of someplace, or someone, to investigate. Being Retta, she couldn't wait for us to return and be her backup.

Impulsive. Headstrong. That was Retta.

Mr. Pretter was out looking for Styx, along with several neighbors. Mrs. Pretter was apologetic. "Of course Newfs dig," she said. "But it's January. We never thought he could tunnel out of that doghouse."

"Styx is a determined guy," I told her. "I'm here to help, if I can."

"You might drive around and call to him," she said. "Maybe he'll respond if he hears a familiar voice."

That's what I did, for over an hour. With Barb's car heater on full blast and my head out the window, I followed country roads for miles, calling for Styx and whistling. I saw dairy farms. I saw buffalo. I saw pretty communities with names unpronounceable to non-Scandinavian folk. I did not see Styx or hear him. When I saw someone outside, I stopped and asked, but no one had seen a big, shaggy dog running free.

All the while I wondered how long I could justify searching for the dog when my sister was in danger. The Pretters would make every effort. Someone might find him and call the number on his tag. Other possibilities weren't as good. He might get hit by a car. He might fall into a lake and get caught under the ice. He might even be mistaken for a bear and shot.

Stop that! I told myself. *He's only been gone a few hours.*

The thought of Retta's heartbreak when she learned her dog was missing made me cringe. Styx was her baby, and when we had to tell her—I stopped myself. At this point I didn't know if we'd ever see Retta again. Losing Styx would be hard for her, but if we were together, the three of us, we'd get through it.

My phone rang, and I pulled onto the side of the road to answer. "Hi, Barb. I haven't found him, but I plan to keep looking until dark—"

"He's here."

"What?"

"He scratched on the door. When I let him in he went right to the bathtub and curled up for a nap."

"Are you sure you want him with us?" I asked when I got back to the motel. Styx was sleeping soundly, making little whistles and snorts. "The kennel people said they could put him in a more secure place."

She chuckled grimly. "Styx wants to be close to Retta. Maybe we'll find a way to put his devotion to use somehow."

CHAPTER EIGHT

BARB

While Faye was gone, I examined everything in the room that belonged to Lars, looking for any clue to what he'd intended when he left Retta alone on Saturday night. There wasn't much to look at: his shaving kit, a gym bag with clean underwear, a rolled t-shirt, and his service weapon, holstered and stored in a side compartment. Unlike most police officers, FBI agents aren't required to be armed at all times. The fact that he'd left his gun behind told me Lars hadn't expected trouble, though I was pretty sure at this point that he'd found it.

When I finished with that, I turned to Retta's things. Where had she gone, and why was she now insisting everything was fine?

Locating her tablet, I checked the history. She hadn't used SIRI since Sunday, so whatever sent her off hadn't come from the internet. I was about to shut it down when I saw a search performed Saturday at 6:47: *National Stolen Art File*. I clicked on that and got a message that informed me I wasn't authorized to access the list. I should contact the nearest FBI office if I had a tip regarding stolen art or cultural property.

Interesting. No doubt Lars was authorized to view the site, and I wondered what he'd looked at there. I guessed the answer was somewhere in the thousands of items gathered at the Critterz Antique & Collectibles Shop.

My phone rang, and the caller ID indicated an Allport number I didn't recognize. Dreading an appeal to extend my car warranty, I answered. "Um, Ms. Evans? This is Wanda, Faye's sister-in-law?"

Though I answered politely, "Oh, hello, Wanda," I caught myself frowning in the mirror. I wasn't impressed with any of Dale's sisters, but Wanda was my least favorite.

"I have a legal question for you."

"I'm retired." It sounded abrupt, but like most lawyers, I get tired of people asking for free legal advice on the most tenuous of connections. Wanda had probably spoken twenty words to me in her life, and she had that way of looking a person up and down like she was mentally listing what she intended to make fun of later.

"Well, I don't know if Faye's told you, but our mom left behind a will that's really strange and completely unfair."

"No." Even if Faye had mentioned it, I wouldn't have admitted it to Wanda.

"She left everything to the church, and that's not right. I mean, isn't it supposed to be the kids that get the estate?"

Estate? Harriet had left a run-down farm house and eighty acres of rocky soil. "That's what wills are for. They say what the owner wants to have happen to her belongings."

"But what if it isn't fair? Is there a way to change it? Can a judge say it has to get done different?" As her tone grew more intense, I pictured Wanda, hair dyed white-blond, eyes ringed with mascara, and lips always in a pout about something. The world was unfair to her. Nobody treated her well. Everything should be different so she could be happy. No matter what changed, she never was.

"You'll have to speak to someone else about this."

"But you're still a lawyer, even if you did retire. You could—"

60

"I'm occupied with something right now. My advice is to consult an attorney in a professional setting." *Maybe he'll have enough integrity to tell you to go fly a kite.*

Her tone turned snide. "Well. I'm sorry if I *bothered* you when you're working on something more important than family. I just thought you'd want to help your sister out, but I guess you don't care about her."

There were so many things I might have said. What I did say was, "You have a nice day, Wanda."

"Why would there be stolen goods in a junky little place like Critterz?" Faye asked when I told her Lars had consulted the FBI's stolen goods database. "Styx, yes, I really am glad to see you." He was showering her with dog kisses, and she patted him absently.

"The simplest answer is that some heir sold an estate to the sisters without realizing there was contraband mixed in."

"Don't they put out lists of stolen goods business owners are supposed to watch for?"

"Yes, but how often do you think shops like Critterz check?"

"So a stolen ring came in, and they put it out for sale. Lars recognized it."

I continued the scenario. "He came back to the room, looked it up on the FBI's list, and told Retta he had to go out again."

"He wanted to make sure he was right before reporting the discovery."

"What happened after that? Why did Lars go missing?"

I took off my glasses and rubbed my forehead. "That's what we need to figure out."

CHAPTER NINE

Retta

When Lydia left me locked in the windowless little room, I went back to the wall and spoke to Lars. "Did you hear that?"

"Most of it."

"What do you think they're going to do with us?"

"I honestly don't know. If they intended to kill me they should have done it by now." That sounded good until he went on. "But they could be waiting for something else to happen before they do it."

"So we aren't going to die today, but we'll probably die soon if we don't do something."

He made a noise that might have been a laugh. "You face things head on, Retta. I like that."

"But I'm right, aren't I? We need to get out of here."

"We do. Are you wearing those boots I like?"

"It's January and we're north of the 45th parallel. Of course I'm wearing boots."

"The wall between us is one layer of planks, and the nail heads face me. Use your heel to kick the end of the bottom board loose."

I didn't object, though I did recognize the permanent damage that would do to my Ferragamo footwear. After bending to feel around until I found the right spot, I turned my back and gave it a good kick. It stung, and at first nothing happened, but a few more kicks and Lars said, "It's coming." Looking down, I saw I'd moved it about a half-inch. Lars couldn't get his fingers into the gap yet, so I kicked a few more times. When the space was wide enough for him to take hold, he pulled on the end while I walloped the middle. My thighs started aching from the strain, I heard the drawn-out creak of the nails at the opposite end breaking loose. One more kick and there was a pop as they released. Lars' grin appeared in the opening. "One down."

We went to work on the next board up, Lars pulling while I kicked. This one was more difficult to strike squarely, being higher, but his pressure added to my impetus, and soon we had an eight-inch gap. Of course the boards were staggered, so the hole was irregular. The third board was more resistant, and Lars applied his weight to the free end and broke it off. It made a splintery mess, but he kicked the jagged ends off, making an opening big enough to allow me a room-to-room shift.

The first thing we did was hug for a while. Lars was dirtier than I, and he looked like he hadn't slept since I last saw him, but it felt good to feel his arms around me, put my head on his broad chest, and hear his strong heartbeat.

After a moment I stepped back to take stock of the place, better lit than my former cell due to a small glass-brick window set a little above my eye level. The twenty-by-thirty area was walled by stone on three sides, which meant it was the westernmost end of the old mill. The plank wall we'd just breached formed part of the fourth wall, and the rest was a stretch of heavy cyclone fencing with a sliding gate in the center secured with a chain and padlock. Along the side walls were items probably destined for the shop upstairs after cleanup or repair. Squinting, I made out a stack of dining chairs, a buffet, an old stereo cabinet, and a drop-leaf table.

Two blankets in the front right corner indicated Lars' primitive living quarters. An electric heater sat outside the fencing, aimed toward it. It didn't warm the space, but I guessed it had kept Lars from freezing to death. Beside the blankets were an empty plate and a coffee cup.

Nothing I saw suggested a way out.

Going to the fencing, I peered into the gloomy expanse beyond it. As my eyes adjusted I discerned the staircase that almost bisected the space. At the opposite end was an area similar to the one we occupied, though the gate at that end stood open. In its back corner were two upright metal posts, the guide rails for the freight elevator. Looking up, I saw the metal base of the car was flush with the showroom floor.

Closer to us were two doors, one to the room I'd just come from. Lars said the other was a bathroom. "I get regular access to it, and they feed me very well." he admitted. "If it weren't for the threat of death, I might stay here just for Betty's tapioca pudding."

Ignoring his attempt at a joke, I said, "The far wall is newer than the rest."

"I noticed. No way do they want their renters snooping in their merchandise, since some of it is stolen."

"And I was stupid enough to fall for their trick."

Lars chuckled. "You aren't the first, trust me." Before I could pursue that subject he asked, "How did you find me?"

"When you didn't come back to the room, I got a text saying you were leaving without me—with another woman."

"I wondered how they'd explain my disappearance." After a beat he asked, "You didn't believe I'd do that, did you?"

65

"Not for a minute. Besides, they spelled out *goodbye*, the whole word."

He chuckled. "Complete words are a dead giveaway that your texter is over sixty."

"Was it DeeAnne and Betty who locked you in?"

"DeeAnne lured me down here and Lydia hit me with something."

"She *hit* you? They just pushed me."

He rubbed his head. "Lydia is one nasty woman. I was dazed for a few seconds, and I felt them sort of steering me forward. When my brain started working again I was locked in here, my phone was gone, and I had a lump the size of a casaba on the side of my head."

I felt the lump, which was still noticeable though no longer melon-sized. "You poor thing! It's a wonder you don't have a concussion."

He chuckled grimly. "Scandinavian hard-head, that's me."

"I can't believe the others would go along with this. DeeAnne is a little drifty but she doesn't seem evil, and Betty? She's a sweetheart."

Lars made a sound of agreement. "It's hard to say how much the older two understand about what's going on, but I think one reason we're still alive is that Lydia knows they wouldn't approve of murder."

"That's something, I guess. But what's going on here that warrants kidnapping an FBI agent?"

"I'm not sure of the details. When we came in on Saturday—" He stopped. "What day is it now?"

"Monday, late afternoon."

He nodded, apparently pleased he'd guessed correctly. "I thought I recognized some pieces in the jewelry case as stolen goods from Iraq. We're encouraged to stay aware of stuff like that, but it had been a while since I checked the FBI's look-out list. Back at the room, I checked your tablet and confirmed my suspicions."

"Really?"

"I figured those women didn't know what they had." With a snort of disgust he added, "That was more wrong than I've ever been before."

"They're quite a trio." That reminded me. "Speaking of trios, Barb and Faye are here. I called them in when the police didn't take your disappearance seriously."

"That's good. They'll pressure the locals to keep looking for us."

"Except Lydia made me say you and I were heading for New Mexico. That gives them, what, two or three days to figure out how to make a plausible exit from Green Bay, probably from the whole state."

Lars set his hands under his arms in an attempt to warm them. "If they announce they're closing the business and retiring to Arizona or somewhere, it will seem legitimate."

"Except we know different." We stared at each other as certainty dawned. "They'll kill us before they go."

Lars pushed that thought away. "Now that you're here, I think we can put a kink in their plans."

"What can I do that you can't?"

He hugged me again. "Let's just say it's a good thing it's not Faye who's locked in here."

CHAPTER TEN

Faye

Barb read me information on the FBI's Art Crime Team, a squad of just over a dozen agents. Established in 2004 after the looting of the Baghdad Museum, their purview was residential and museum thefts, both foreign and domestic. With the unenviable job of trying to track down the more than four to six billion dollars' worth of art stolen and resold each year in the U.S., they were called in any time it was determined contraband had crossed state lines.

"I wonder, did Lars report what he'd found or just check the list?"

As if in answer to her question, a knock sounded on the door. I rose to answer and found a woman, neatly but plainly dressed, with a blunt haircut and pink eyeglasses that brought Randy Rainbow to mind. Her clothes, glasses, and scowling expression didn't completely conceal her attractiveness, though I guessed it was an attempt to be taken seriously by both criminals and co-workers. Holding up a wallet with a gold badge that said *Federal Bureau of Investigation* on one side and an I.D. card on the other, she announced, "Agent Stiles from the Green Bay office. I'm looking for Margaretta Stilson."

"She's not here, but we're her sisters. What's this about?"

Stiles made a quick survey of the room, as if distrustful of my honesty. "She called the FBI about the disappearance of an agent. I'm here to follow up on that."

Relief flooded through me but Barb, less trusting than I, joined me at the doorway. "May I see your credentials again?"

The woman held up the wallet but didn't offer to let her take it, which I knew was correct procedure. After having Lars around for a couple of years, we knew a little about what gave an agent legitimacy. The badge was the proper size and shape, and it had *Department of Justice* in embossed letters at the bottom.

Stowing the badge she said, "I'm hoping this is a mix-up."

"Well, it isn't." When Barb filled her in on Lars' disappearance and our discovery that Retta was now gone too, Stiles frowned. "It's out of character for her to travel on to her original destination without seeing you personally?"

"It's out of character for her to leave her tablet, her makeup, and her dog behind." Barb glanced toward the bathroom, where Styx, aware we had a visitor, had begun making a racket. "Retta's Newfoundland is like her child. She wouldn't leave him, even with us."

"She has a dog?"

Going to the door I pushed it open, which wasn't easy with Styx pressing from the other side, and caught his collar before he could launch himself at Stiles. He wanted to, but I set my feet and held onto the door frame. "This is Styx. Retta loves him to death."

"I see." After a moment she said, "I'll make some inquiries."

Barb said what I hoped she'd say. "We can help, Agent Stiles. We're trained investigators."

Stiles' eyes flashed, which I guessed meant *Not now, not ever*. What she said was, "I think you'll find you can't legally begin an investigation in a state other than your own."

"But Retta's our sister."

"And Johannsen is one of ours. I'll do everything possible to find them, but they're probably somewhere in Kansas, doing exactly what Ms. Stilson told you they'd do."

"Not without Styx." I hadn't meant to say it aloud. It just came out.

Stiles' mouth hardened. "What if the dog was the point of contention? What if Johannsen decided he can't live with an animal that big and, um, energetic?"

Time spent in a motel room with Styx would be an eye-opener, for sure. There'd also been some discussion of his adjustment to an apartment, since Styx had always had a whole house, a big yard, and no one but Retta around when he decided to bark just to hear his own voice. Lars had said they'd make it work. Might he have reconsidered in the harsh light of reality?

"So Lars texted a lie to Retta, took off, then came back when she agreed to give up her dog in order to live with him? No." Barb made a cutting gesture. "He'd wait to see how things worked out."

"And if he *had* decided he couldn't live with Styx," I added, "Retta would have turned around and gone back to Michigan."

The agent seemed unconvinced. "You say she called you and indicated things were fine."

"There's something else," Barb picked up Retta's tablet and opened the search history. "Lars looked at the NSAF website just before he disappeared. I think he spotted something he thought was stolen art."

"Where would he have seen something like that around here?"

I handed her one of the fliers I'd taken from a table at the Old Mill and pointed at the listing for Critterz. "Retta thought Lars' mood changed when they visited this shop."

"All right." The agent's gaze moved from Barb to me. "What I need you to do is monitor your phones. Ms. Stilson will probably call again when they stop for the night, so we'll get a location." We had to admit that was true. "I'll give you my direct line." She moved toward a note pad lying next to the bedside lamp. Unfortunately, she stepped into Styx's personal space, and my grip had relaxed a little. He lunged into her, knocking her against the stand.

As her thigh hit the edge, Stiles said a socially unacceptable word. I made allowances, since a nudge from Styx can result in anything from a red mark to a broken bone. Apparently she was okay, and after a brief period of rubbing, managed to complete the task she'd begun. "Call if you hear from either of them."

"Is there anything else we can do?" I asked.

"I'll be sure to let you know if there is." A twitch of her lips betrayed her real thought, which I read as, *Stay out of my way.*

Chapter Eleven

Barb

The first thing I did when Agent Stiles left was look up the local FBI office on line. They listed three agents on staff, and one was Jamie Stiles. There were no photos, but it said Stiles had been in Wisconsin for four years.

I filled Rory in by phone. "It's nice to know the Bureau is on the case," he said.

"Yes, but I got a distinct sense of law enforcement attitude from Stiles. 'You're amateurs. Back off.'"

"Not all cops see you that way," Rory responded. "You made believers out of everybody over here."

"Well, we're starting all over again here. Middle-aged. Women. Probably menopausal." I glanced at Faye, who nodded vigorously. "We both sensed the agent has no time for us."

"If it makes you feel any better, I faced a bit of ageism myself this weekend. A teeny-bopper took one of the county plow-trucks for a joy-ride and got busted. When we brought the parents in, the mother, who's all of thirty-five, told me I'd probably done the same thing back in my day, but I'm too old to remember."

"And you said?"

"That if I'd done the stunt her son pulled, I'd have accepted the punishment the law doled out, and my parents would have added a few twists of their own to be sure I got the message."

"Did she get *your* message?"

"Not even close. I'm sure there's a poorly spelled rant about the Allport City Police on social media by now."

"Not much you can do about that."

"Nope. Online ranters don't have to abide by rules, good taste, or common sense."

"People who know you will know better."

"Probably." That was all he had to say on that topic. "Social media might help us find Retta though. You could post a photo and ask for sightings on the highway between Wisconsin and New Mexico."

"How would we do that?"

"I can handle it. It will make me feel like I'm helping. I'll track down any leads we get too." He chuckled. "I'll warn you. Ninety percent of the reports will be from men who claim they spent last night with Retta and had the time of their lives."

"Ick!"

"It's what happens. People love drama, and if they aren't part of it, they're liable to make something up."

"Let's focus on Retta. I doubt the FBI wants us publicizing the unconfirmed disappearance of one of their agents."

"Okay." Briefly we discussed what needed to be done. I had a recent photo of Retta on my phone. Rory would present it online not as a police request, but as a "need to contact" from family. He'd look up Retta's license plate number and post a vehicle's description. His office would monitor responses and follow up on those that might be legitimate. If Retta and Lars were on the road, someone would see them and report it.

And if Retta really was okay, she was going to want to kill me for making her trip to New Mexico go viral.

CHAPTER TWELVE

Retta

I examined the window Lars thought I could escape through. It wasn't very big, and I wondered how we'd remove the glass bricks without tools. "I assume you looked for other ways out?"

"I tried pounding on the glass to attract attention. No luck. At daylight on Sunday, I shoved the loose papers I had in my pockets out through this crack between the window frame and the wall." He pointed to a slit about three inches long and just wide enough for paper. "I hoped it would catch someone's attention, but it didn't."

"Actually, it did. Barbara found our restaurant receipt while she was doing one of her little 'policing the area' maneuvers. That's how we knew you came back here."

"Good. That will give the police a place to focus on."

"But they checked here once. We can't wait for them to get around to a second visit."

"No. Tonight after the White sisters go up to their apartment, we'll start hacking at those bricks and see if we can displace them."

I snuggled close to him, sharing body heat. "While we wait, tell me what you know about what's going on here."

"As I said, I was pretty sure I'd seen some of the items offered for sale upstairs before. They're part of 10,000 pieces stolen from the Bagdad Museum in Iraq in 2003."

"Stuff that was taken when everything was a mess over there."

"Right. In the chaos, nobody protected the nation's antiquities, and we know of three separate robberies at the museum. The FBI Director during that time, Robert Mueller, vowed we'd find and return what we could of items that came to the U.S."

"So how did Iraqi treasures get to Green Bay, Wisconsin?"

"That's the question that made me doubt myself, and I was afraid that if I was wrong, I'd get razzed for suspecting a trio of senior citizens. Once I checked the list, I was pretty sure it was the same jewelry, so I came back to get a closer look."

"And got locked in the basement. How did that happen?"

"I suppose you could blame years of indoctrination as a Southern gentleman." I heard the humor in Lars' voice, though I could no longer see his features clearly. "That little old lady got me good."

"Her name is DeeAnne," I supplied.

"I don't know how she got suspicious of me, but she did."

A stab of guilt hit as I remembered mentioning to her that my companion was an FBI agent. I shouldn't do that, but it's fun to watch people's eyes widen when I say it. Lars didn't need to know I'd outed him, so I said nothing.

"She was sweet as pie when I asked to see those pieces close up. When I mentioned provenance, she said they're very careful about it."

I huffed in disgust. "Except when they can sell it at a good profit!"

"Anyway, I kept it casual. I even bought an antique toy that I said was for my grandson. As I was about to leave, she asked if I'd help her out by carrying a box downstairs. She's pretty tiny, and she played the helpless damsel. I fell for it.'"

"It was a trap."

"Yes. While I was looking at the jewelry, she'd made a phone call. What she said didn't sound threatening, just something like, 'I think I'll close early tonight. I have some things to do downstairs if you'd like to meet me there.' She told the other person to bring something, I think she said *knobkerrie*, but I didn't know what that was." He touched his head again. "I'm going to guess it's some kind of weapon."

"Zulu war club," I murmured. Despite Barbara Ann's disdain for them, romance novels can expand a person's vocabulary. "Lydia was waiting when you got down here."

"To my everlasting chagrin." He grimaced. "Beaned and imprisoned by a couple of senior citizens. I'll never live it down."

"Don't worry," I told him. "When they go upstairs this evening, you'll get me out of here. It will be my pleasure me to set the police on those vicious old bats."

CHAPTER THIRTEEN

Faye

Rory's suggestion of putting out a call on social media at least made me feel like we were doing something. I sent him a half-dozen photos of Retta and Retta's SUV, the best ones I could find on my phone.

It wasn't enough to calm me down. If Lars had been kidnapped (or killed!) by some old enemy, and Retta had somehow tracked that person down, she was obviously his prisoner. He'd made her call to throw us off the trail, and though it hadn't worked, I couldn't see what our next move should be. We weren't about to leave Retta's fate in the hands of an FBI agent who thought she knew the answers without really asking any questions.

I kept imagining our sister in dire situations. Was she locked in the trunk of a car, speeding away from Green Bay to some remote destination where she'd be shot and left in a shallow grave? Was she tied up in some motel room while Lars' killer decided how he was going to dispose of her? Maybe she'd escaped somehow and was running through snowdrifts to try to find help.

I called Dale to check in, and though he tried to be casual, little things he said came across as warnings. "I heard there's been a rash of burglaries in Green Bay. Hope Barb remembers to lock her car."

"Barb always remembers, Hon. She lived in the big city far too long to forget."

"How's she doing with Styx?"

"Retta fixed him a place in the bathroom, with a towel in the bathtub and his food and water dish under the sink. Styx prefers to be where we are, and since he tends to chase his dishes around as he eats, they end up underfoot. I can see Barb trying to be patient with spilled water and kibble in the corners."

"Sounds like Styx is a problem."

"Let's just say they challenge each other. He doesn't understand why she doesn't think he's wonderful, and she doesn't understand why he hasn't got a scrap of dignity. But we'll manage. How's Buddy handling my absence?"

"He grudgingly accepts me as a poor substitute for you."

"I know you're fibbing. Buddy loves you because you play the oldies for him."

He chuckled. "We do get down some: Aerosmith, the Doobie Brothers, a little Smokey Robinson."

Suddenly I missed Dale more than I could bear. "I wish—" It hung in the airwaves between us.

"I know. I hate being the guy who can't come over there and help. You're scared for Retta, and I feel like I should do something about it."

"Oh, Dale. Don't think of it that way. I am scared, but there isn't a single thing you could do if you came. We're here, and we don't know what to do next."

"You'll think of something. You're smart and resourceful."

"There!" I told him. "Just when I start doubting myself, you say something like that and I think, 'If Dale believes that, it must be true.'"

"I'm never wrong," he said firmly. "Not when it comes to you."

"How are things with the family?"

"I don't know whether to laugh or cry," he replied. "It was suggested today that the church should donate Mom's money back to us and call it a charitable act."

"Which genius came up with that one?"

"Elanna, but they're all a little loony on the subject, especially Wanda. They'd have been mad if she split the money evenly among us, or if she gave it all to the eldest or the youngest, or if she spent it on a fancy mausoleum for herself. They just like being mad."

"They'll calm down eventually."

"I know. It's just hard to see your family scrapping like wolves over a few dollars." Dale turned to his favorite subject. "I saw on the news that you guys are getting some bitter cold. I hope you have enough warm clothes."

I was tempted to mention they had stores in Green Bay, but instead said, "I'll bundle up when we go outside. I promise."

I'd just ended the call with Dale when the phone rang again. The caller ID said *Wanda*, and I groaned aloud. Past experience had taught that if I didn't answer, Dale's sister would call again in five minute intervals until I did. Best to get it over.

"Hello."

"Faye, it's Wanda. I've been talking to the others, and we wondered if you and Dale might go in with us and get a lawyer."

"For what?"

"Ma wasn't in her right mind when she wrote that will. If we all say that to the lawyer, we'll get what's owed to us." She paused then added meaningfully, "All of us would get a little money, including you guys."

"Did you speak to Dale about this?"

She didn't answer directly, which I took to mean no. He'd be reluctant to go against his mother's wishes, so she wanted me to approach him. "We all thought you and him should talk it over, you know, together."

"I'd rather not interfere in your family business."

"You're family too, Faye. You guys have been married forever."

And "you guys" never once made me feel welcome.

"I'm sorry, Wanda. I can't do it. You'll have to talk to Dale yourself."

Her voice turned cool. "I was just trying to cut you in. If we break the will and you don't help, you might not get a share."

"I can live with that. Goodbye, Wanda."

Chapter Fourteen

Barb

I'm usually the one who paces, but this time it was Faye who couldn't keep still. Her restlessness made Styx nervous, and he followed her back and forth along the tiny space between the bed and dresser. In seconds everything that wasn't fastened down was on the floor, on its side, or behind the dresser.

"Why don't you take that monster for a walk before it gets too dark?" My tone was harsher than normal, but I was upset too.

She was so distracted she didn't notice my irritation. "I can do that."

She got Styx's leash and hooked it to his collar, which started a whole new round of dog-tremors around the room. "I noticed a park about two blocks that way," I told her. "It edges the river."

"That means you stay on the leash," she told him. If allowed to run, Styx might come back wet despite the cold. Newfs love the water, and they don't think outside is fun until the temperature drops below freezing.

Once they were gone and I could think, I went over our options. We could do as we were told and hang out in our miniature motel room, which would drive us both crazy. We could manufacture some sort of activity, like shopping at the mall or gambling at a casino. Those things didn't appeal to either of us at the best of times, much less when we were missing a sibling. Or we could investigate on our own. That's the option I chose, and though Faye would hate it that I left her behind, I had one advantage she didn't. The ladies at the antique shop had never seen me. If they were innocent dupes of some art thief, a visit from me might glean information that would help us find Retta. If they weren't as innocent as they appeared, a stranger might discover that with carefully posed questions. Checking the clock, I saw I had time for a visit before they closed for the day. I left Faye a note, warmed up my car for a couple of minutes, and left.

Critterz was like a lot of other shops I'd seen that bill themselves as sellers of antiques but mostly deal in vintage junk. The idea that the owners engaged in criminal activity seemed ludicrous with a row of He-Man toys fronting the first aisle. Beyond Skeletor was a set of depression-glass serving dishes with a cracked pitcher. Stacked against the wall were straight chairs of a dozen different types, no more than three of any one kind. And there were the inevitable metal tins, some with names like *Whitman* or *Tetley's*, others with painted flowers or Christmas scenes.

Weaving toward the back, I tried not to be deterred by items that would have interested me in other circumstances. Would those chrome mirrors fit my '57 Chevy? Mine were a little pitted from Michigan weather, though I always put the car in storage before the first snowflake fell. *Keep walking!* And that apron looked just like one Mom always wore on Thanksgiving. *Focus!* Ignoring the rest, I went on.

The back wall of the store had once been the control center of the flour mill. A dozen electrical switches, each three feet high, had been left in place to create atmosphere and interest. To the left of a long counter was a freight elevator with a large sign that warned people to stay off. To my right was a doorway marked *Staff Only*. A large antique cash register and the only modern items in the place, a computer, a credit card reader, and a cell phone, topped the counter. Behind it was a woman with hair much too black to be natural and a brow full of wrinkles from a lifetime of frowning. She looked up with neither interest nor welcome. In a voice like a school bell she said, "Yes?"

"I'm looking for something special in the way of jewelry for my daughter's birthday, vintage stuff." When she merely looked at me I added, "She's going to be thirty, so it's kind of a big deal."

Her expression said thirty wasn't *that* big a deal, and I had to agree, thirty looks pretty good from the other side of fifty. I hoped that if she was crooked and a little dumb, I'd get a look at stuff regular customers didn't see.

"This is what we got." The faint trace of Scandinavia, fairly common in the Upper Midwest, colored her pronunciation of *what* and *got*. A precise *t* at the end, not just a glottal stop.

I pretended to consider. "I was hoping for something unique."

"This is all there is." Her tone said, *Take it or leave it. I don't care.*

I hadn't really thought she'd show a tray of stolen goods to a stranger. "This place is cute. Do you run it by yourself?"

"There's three of us." The *h* was almost missing from *three*.

"Have you been here long?"

"Long enough." Her manner had gone from cool politeness to irritation. I couldn't tell whether I'd given myself away somehow or she was just a naturally unfriendly type.

Faint heart never won fair information. "How do you make sure the stuff isn't stolen?"

Her dark eyes got darker. "Everything you see here is legitimate."

"I didn't mean you'd sell contraband on purpose, but if you buy an estate and sell it off piece by piece, how do you know one of those pieces isn't from a robbery a decade ago?"

She shrugged. "There are lists online."

"But with so much stuff it must be hard to keep up."

She glanced around the room. "We're careful. Stolen goods get confiscated, so you're out the money you spent."

"Oh. It's kind of a risk then, selling secondhand."

She met my gaze. "Not unless you're sloppy."

A rattle to my left startled me, and I turned to see the freight elevator rising. I watched with interest as it disappeared into the ceiling. A few seconds later it came back down, carrying the woman Faye had described. She wore a gypsy-type skirt in greens and blues with a black leotard top. Over her shoulders was a short cape in colors that varied from red to purple. "Lydia," she called, "Betty needs your help for a minute. I can wait on this lady while you're gone."

"Good luck." I didn't know whether that was a criticism of me, DeeAnne, or both of us. Opening the *Staff Only* door, Lydia took the stairs rather than the elevator.

DeeAnne approached, her cape fluttering as she pranced dramatically forward. I gestured at the elevator. "Quite a contraption."

"I love it," DeeAnne said. "Every time I press the button, I feel like Phileas Fogg flying off in his balloon to go around the world." While everything Lydia had said was terse and flat-toned, DeeAnne's statements were more suited to '30s movie dialogue.

"I'm surprised it still works. It must be decades since it was used to move flour."

"Our Max, he's Lydia's grandson, is clever with machinery. He got it going with a little oil and a few new parts."

85

"You should give rides. Parents would pay to let their kids try it."

"It doesn't go anywhere interesting," she objected. "Upstairs is our home, which we prefer to keep private. Downstairs is storage, not pretty." She waved a hand. "Now what were you interested in?"

"Some unique piece of jewelry for my daughter's thirtieth birthday." I looked down at the case between us. "Nothing here caught my eye. I asked the other lady if there were other, um, items that weren't on display. Special things."

"Oh, no. We never hold things back." She sounded genuinely shocked. "That wouldn't be fair to our customers."

"Thanks. I'll just look around, see if anything catches my eye."

"Enjoy!" DeeAnne said breezily, and I moved away, wandering the many pathways available. Unsure what I was looking for, I moved slowly through the store, taking in Kewpie dolls and ancient magazines, battered sleds and the old kind of ice cube trays with a lever. As I went I encountered no less than four cats, all of whom seemed uninterested in my presence. I petted one, a long-haired gray, and spoke to the others, who perched on cabinets or fixtures above me, looking down on humans, as cats like to do.

As I walked my phone pulsed, and I saw it was Faye. *Whr R U?*

I answered, *Junk shop. Back soon.*

As I put the phone away, I heard voices at the counter. Lydia had returned, and the sound of the elevator told me DeeAnne was on her way back to the apartment. The new speaker was a man, youngish, with what I think of as a city accent. "—really need to talk to Kye." Sidling to the end of the aisle, I peered around an armoire to get a look at him. He was handsome in a slightly wolfish way, with lots of black hair pulled into a knot atop his head and teeth that flashed white as he talked. It was hard to tell much more about him from a side view, but his clothes seemed juvenile, like he hadn't yet grown out of trendy-but-not-necessarily-attractive choices. The flat, black-and-white Converse shoes he wore weren't much protection in a Wisconsin January.

Lydia's voice was cold. "My grand-daughter goes where she pleases. I'm not informed."

"But you work for her, so you must know where she is."

There was a pause that practically crackled with outrage before Lydia said, "I work *with* Kylie, not *for* her."

"Whatever. Her and me were real tight down in Madison, and then one day she just up and left. I need to find her." His voice turned ominous as he added, "The cops questioned her about the death of a certain customer. She came out of it okay, but there are things they didn't hear about."

All he got for that was a sniff, and he seemed unsure how to proceed. After a few seconds he said, "If she don't make things right, I'll tell the cops what I heard her say to you on the phone."

I wouldn't have guessed Lydia's tone could get any colder, but it did. "I'll inform Kylie that you're in town. There's a lot going on right now, but I'm sure she'll look you up when time permits."

"I'll give her a day." Pulling out his phone, he checked the time. "Four o'clock tomorrow, I go to the cops. If she did what I think she did, I ain't gettin' caught up in it—unless I get some incentive to keep quiet." He turned to go, and I wondered how he withstood the malevolent gaze Lydia focused on his back. Following discreetly, I watched as he got into an old Crown Vic that looked like it might once have been a police car.

Starting it up, he put it into gear, resulting in a series of jerks that smoothed out once the wheels got rolling.

"Excuse me." I turned to find a thirty-something man in Carhartts carrying an old sewing machine. I backed down a side aisle to get out of his way and then, realizing he was heading outside, moved ahead to open the door for him. By the time he'd passed me, the guy in the Crown Vic had joined the flow of traffic on the street. It was too late to follow and question him.

The store employee—Was he the Max DeeAnne had mentioned?—loaded the old Singer onto a flatbed truck. Looking up, he gave me a smile that seemed smug, like he thought he'd done something clever. Getting into the truck, he drove away as I stood for a few seconds, going over in my mind what I'd heard.

Someone had died. The police had questioned Lydia's granddaughter. The guy with the man-bun knew things that would make trouble for Lydia's grand-daughter.

This place was more than a second-hand shop, and these women were more than purveyors of junk. I needed to get Faye working on finding out more about them.

Picking up the first small item at hand, I went to the counter. "I'll take this."

"Huh." Lydia seemed to take interest in me for the first time. "Wouldn't have pegged you for a Holly Hobbie collector."

Faye wasn't pleased that I'd gone to the old mill alone. "What would I have done if you disappeared too?" she chided.

"I was careful," I told her, "and you're better at keeping Styx happy than I am." The dog sensed my lack of enthusiasm for his shenanigans, and while he was willing to forgive and forget, I kept my distance when possible. That made Faye his favorite aunt by far.

Grudgingly she accepted my arguments, and I went on to describe the man I'd seen. "Might he be FBI?" Faye asked. "Stiles might have send someone in under cover."

"I didn't get the impression she was working with anyone."

Faye nodded. "I wish we could ask, but then she'd know we've been snooping."

"Not snooping," I corrected. "Even if our license isn't valid here, we have the right as private citizens to look for our sister."

Faye came as close as she ever does to voicing criticism. "I wish you'd caught up with that guy and asked what he knows. We need to figure this out if we're going to find Retta and Lars."

CHAPTER FIFTEEN

Retta

As we waited for our captors' last visit of the day, Lars and I got ready for my escape. Lars used a coin from his pocket to unscrew a metal brace from a chest of drawers, a make-shift chisel for the mortar. I found a couple of table leaves that raised him a few inches so he could work at a comfortable level. When the elevator roared to life, I scurried back through the hole we'd made in the wall, and Lars set a box in place to cover it.

It was Betty, who warned through the door that Lydia was at the top of the stairs, ready to shoot us if we tried to escape. Sounds indicated she'd unlocked the gate to the fenced area, and she said, "Mr. Johannsen, go ahead and eat while I take Ms. Stilson to the ladies' room." My door opened, and she indicated I should lead the way.

The "ladies room" wasn't suitable for ladies: an ancient toilet, a rust-stained sink, and a roll of paper set on a tank laced with spider webs and dead flies. Luckily, the spider didn't seem to be home. My bladder had been telling me for some time that it needed relief, so I took advantage, doing my best not to touch anything with any part of me. When I finished, the flush was so loud I jumped a foot, but at least I had one less stressor.

I attempted the divide-and-conquer technique common in crime-fighting. "Betty, do you know that your sister is breaking the law?"

Her answer surprised me. "Oh, yes, dear. She's quite good at it."

"But you and DeeAnne could be charged as accomplices. You've kidnapped a federal agent, and now me. You started this business with lots of hard work. She uses it to commit crimes."

Her oversized dentures flashed in the dim light. "I did start it, and what did I get? I practically starved through the winters. Lydia took things in hand and made a success of it."

"Moving stolen goods under the cover of your good name."

Betty gave a little shrug. "For years I was alone, always on the edge of bankruptcy, and every single decision was up to me. Do you know how hard it is to have no one to talk to—no one you can even ask, 'Should I sell the Depression glass or hold it in hopes the price will go up?' Now I've got my sisters, and there's money. I've been happier in the last ten years than in my whole life before."

Having no argument to counter that, I went meekly back to my cell. Once I was locked in, Lars was allowed to use the facilities while I ate a pork chop dinner complete with potatoes, gravy, corn, and a fat dinner roll. Betty locked him in again then came to get my dishes. "Here's a treat for later," she said, handing me a zipper bag containing two peanut butter cookies. "I just made them."

I thanked her, though it was strange to express gratitude to someone keeping us prisoner. At the sound of the elevator rising, Lars moved the box away from the hole in the wall and I crawled back to his side. Taking a cookie from his treat bag, he ate it in two bites then brushed the crumbs from his hands. "Let's get those bricks out."

Lars dug patiently at the mortar for what seemed like hours, but eventually one brick started to wiggle. Soon after that it separated from the others, giving us a blast of cold air and a view to the outside. We peered out to see an old PT Cruiser, some trash bins filled to overflowing with items piled around their outsides, and a few snow-covered, scrubby trees, all backed by a fence that proclaimed *Leon's Salvage and Recycling*. In the glow of the security light, I noticed Lars' knuckles were bleeding. Taking off my gloves I ordered, "Put these on. They'll give you a little protection from scrapes."

The gloves were stretchy, and he managed to get his big paw inside one of them. The other he handed back to me, and I put it on to warm my chilly hand. He returned to work, loosening another brick and handing it to me. With one gone, the rest came out more easily.

When the hole was big enough Lars said, "Do you want to go feet first or head?"

"Feet. I'll sit in the opening then roll onto my stomach and lower myself down."

We'd already talked about what I'd do when I was free: hurry to the nearest open business, probably a gas station, and call the police. "Tell them to come in Code One, without lights and sirens," Lars said. "That should get me out before Lydia has a chance to shoot me."

I didn't like the idea of leaving Lars locked in alone for even a few minutes, but it was a small window. "I'll be quick," I promised.

He lifted me, and I put my feet through the narrow hole. It was a tight fit, and I heard a seam in my sleeve rip as it caught on a ragged edge. When I turned, a button from my blouse flew off. I scooted myself out, stretching my feet to reach the ground. When I was almost there, a sound behind me froze us both. "What was that?" Lars asked.

I blocked his view, and I faced him, half in and half out of the window. "It sounds like a truck."

A diesel, from the smell. With a final thrust of my legs, I dropped to the ground, staggered back a step, and turned to see a flatbed truck that had just pulled up. A man in Carhartts got out of it, and I hurried toward him. "Please, I need your help."

"What?" He seemed stunned.

"My friend and I were captured by the criminals who own this building."

The surprised look faded as I spoke, and a sly grin replaced it. "Criminals, eh? My gram and her sisters won't like you spreading that idea one bit."

CHAPTER SIXTEEN

Faye

I like working on a PC with a big screen and all the functions I'm used to right there in the taskbar, but I had to be content with what I had, my phone and Retta's tablet. Laboriously typing on the tiny keys, I looked into the backgrounds of the women who owned Critterz Collections. *Betty White* is a common name, and *Betty* is usually a nickname, so when I typed *Elizabeth White* in the Brown County records, several entries came up. Using a probable birth date of 1938, I narrowed it down to what had to be the correct one. Her address, 188 Barry Street, was where the Old Mill Mall was located. As I clicked on this site and that, Betty's life unfolded. She'd never married, had lived all her life in Green Bay, and worked for thirty years as receptionist and shipping manager at the mill, which had been owned and operated by her uncle until it closed down in the mid-eighties. She had a Facebook page where she listed herself as a "Packer-Backer" (which I assumed meant the football team); a Hank Williams, Sr. groupie; and a "lover of kitty-cats of all kinds."

Finding DeeAnne was easy, since she and Betty were connected on Facebook. Listed as DeeAnne March, though I found no record of her marriage, the middle White sister had lived all over the country, plying a modestly successful career in small theater. She had a self-maintained website with photos, reviews, and congratulatory messages from fans who loved her as Maria von Trapp or Molly Brown. Most of them were from the last century, and over time the roles had changed from ingénue to matron, Snow White to Aunt Flora. Her last entry was in 2007, when she'd managed a nice role for her swan song: Dolly Levi in *Hello, Dolly!* in Dothan, Alabama. Pictures from the production revealed clunky sets and poorly-made costumes, but the players' enthusiasm apparently made up for that. All the posted reviews were positive.

DeeAnne had one child, Roderick, who lived in New York City and was apparently pursuing his own dreams of stardom under the name Roddy McUsher. There were several studio portraits of him on his (much more professional) website, but the roles he'd gleaned in decades of off-off-Broadway productions were minor, starting out as the second-best friend of the lead and trending lately to such roles as the wise old uncle. Roddy seldom commented on his mother's posts; mostly he just "liked" them.

Next I looked for information on Lydia, the sister I had yet to meet. She wasn't on any social media I could find, but her name did show up on sites for "professional resellers" with names like "VintageRUs" and "Selly-How." Listed as *Lydia Peete, manager at Critterz*, she didn't contribute much in the way of commentary but offered merchandise weekly. Critterz also had an on-line store, well-conceived and easy to navigate, with photos, descriptions, and asking prices included. I wondered how three Golden Agers kept track of all that technology, but that was probably an ageist question. It isn't only the young who can learn new things.

Inputting *Lydia Peete* into Brown County records, I confirmed that she lived at the same address as Betty and DeeAnne, had been married once long ago and divorced a few years later. In 2001 her only daughter, Meredith Hayworth, had died in a car accident along with her husband, and at fifty-something, Lydia had taken on the job of raising a ten-year-old grandson, Max, and his seven-year-old sister, Kylie.

Going to a website we use to run background checks, I entered the names of each sister. No arrests or convictions.

The phone rang in my hand, and I almost dropped it. When I found the right button to answer, I heard a timid voice. "Faye? It's Elanna."

Dale's youngest sister was a pale redhead who always seemed tired to the point of exhaustion. Sighing on the inside I said, "Hey, Elanna. What's up?"

"Not much. I just hadn't talked with you for a while, and I thought I'd check in and see if things are okay."

Not even close, but I wasn't about to share with Dale's family that I was in Green Bay, looking for my sister. Had Elanna seen it online and called to get the juicy details?

"We, um, we wondered what you thought about Ma's will."

We told me that the call was not about Retta. Dale's sisters were focused on their own concern, which was getting a share of Harriet's estate. "I don't have an opinion, Elanna. Harriet made the will, and it was her right to do as she liked with her house."

"But we grew up in it. Our childhood home should be ours."

I could have asked two pointed questions: first, why she'd never visited the place if it had been so dear to her, and second, was she interested in living out in the country in a run-down firetrap. I knew better than to do anything more than hum sympathetically.

"I know the house isn't worth much, but somebody might want the land for farming or maybe even to build some nice houses on. If we're willing to hang onto it for a while, the property value could really rise."

"That's not what the will stipulates."

"I know, but maybe we could have a lawyer take a look at it. If we all agree that Ma didn't mean for us to be disinherited, we could do something about it."

I saw Wanda's heavy hand in this. Elanna was the weakest of the four sisters, the one who could be bullied into anything. She was my favorite, though that wasn't saying much. She didn't judge others as harshly as her sisters, and she didn't start things. Her biggest problem was that she couldn't say no.

"Elanna, I've got a lot going on right now. You can tell Wanda you talked to me, but I'm not interested in breaking the will or trying to convince Dale to do it."

"Oh. Well—"

"Sweetie, I have to go. We'll have lunch soon."

That's the kind of lie a person has to tell when her husband has scatterbrains for siblings.

Foot-stomping sounded outside the door, and Barb and Styx came in from their walk, Styx looking exhilarated and Barb looking frazzled. "I just got a call from the Green Bay Police Department. That woman at Critterz called to complain that we've been bothering them."

"What?"

"The officer was polite, but he said the women are 'concerned' because we seem 'fixated' on them for reasons they don't understand."

"Did you tell him about the receipt we found in their parking lot?"

"I did." Her lower lip pressed upward. "He asked if I'd gone to the store in disguise. In *disguise,* for Pete's sake!"

"That's what they told him?"

"I guess so. I argued that incognito isn't the same as in disguise, but I could tell he thought I was splitting hairs."

"So what did he want us to do?"

Her voice turned masculine and fatherly. "'Leave those old women alone. They're respectable business owners, and what you did might be interpreted as harassment.'" She shook her head. "Just for entering their store and making conversation!"

"I wonder how they figured out you were family to Retta."

"There was a man working in the store. I think he was the guy who was outside smoking when you asked that other shop owner about seeing Lars. He saw us all together."

She nodded. "That's probably it." After a second she said, "Respectable business owners don't have two people disappear immediately after visiting their store. What did you find out about those women?"

As I told her, Barb's expression showed disappointment. I ended with, "Honestly, I have a hard time imagining them as criminals. Like the cop said, they've been in business here for decades. And they're what I think of as *senior* senior citizens."

Barb dropped onto the bed and tugged off her boots. "In the D.A.'s office, we dealt with plenty of elderly crooks. Some people always want what they shouldn't have, and they're willing to do whatever it takes to get it."

CHAPTER SEVENTEEN

Retta

The driver I'd hoped would be my rescuer reached into the side compartment of his truck door and took out a tire iron. "Don't do anything dumb, or I'll brain you."

From the glassless window Lars hollered, "You hurt her and I'll tear you to pieces!"

"Shut up or you'll get the same!" Pulling out a phone, the guy punched a few buttons then put it near his mouth like he was holding a plate of cookies. "Gram? You'd better get out to the back, and bring the gun."

When Lydia appeared a few minutes later, wrapped in a fuzzy bathrobe, a dog on guard at the junk yard next door had begun barking excitedly. Peering down at us from the platform, she held the pistol at her side, hiding it from casual view. She spoke firmly to the unseen dog. "Quiet, Brutus!" Surprisingly, the creature obeyed.

Next Lydia addressed the man. "It's lucky you came along when you did, Max."

He was eager to tell his story. "She come runnin' up to me like I was gonna save her butt." I wanted to kick him in the shins—or higher—but common sense kept me still. I saw Lars at the window, his expression concerned.

"Close up that hole." Lydia ordered, her tone not much different with Max than it had been with the junkyard dog. She started down the steps. "I'll take her back inside."

Max looked around. "I'll use boards off that dresser we threw away."

"Good." To me she said, "Upstairs."

I was halfway up when the door opened and DeeAnne and Betty stepped onto the porch. Betty wore a faded man's flannel bathrobe; DeeAnne had thrown a sweater over a full-length silk nightgown that brought to mind a Joan Crawford movie. "What's she doing out here?"

"Got out through the window." Max had begun breaking the back off the old dresser. "I come along and caught her."

"Keep your voice down." Lydia surveyed the area nervously. Max was a less cautious henchman than a trio of criminals might wish for.

DeeAnne opened the door. When we were back inside she said, "We'd have been in a terrible mess if Maxie hadn't come along."

"We're still in a mess," Lydia growled. "We have been ever since Betty let a frigging FBI agent see the Iraqi stuff."

"I'm sorry," Betty interjected. "I forgot it was your special stock."

"DeeAnne should have noticed."

That brought an outraged huff from DeeAnne. "I can't watch her all the time."

"What else do I ask you to do?" Lydia didn't allow her sister to reply. "I took care of the guy and covered his absence. We had time to get things wrapped up, but you two locked the girlfriend up too!"

DeeAnne looked pouty. "You locked him up; we locked her up. Why is okay when you do it but not when we do?"

"Because one abrupt disappearance might be voluntary. It's a lot harder to float that explanation when a second person goes missing."

Betty spoke soothingly. "We'll be ready to leave for Arizona soon. Then we can let them go, just like you said."

There was a slight hesitation before Lydia said, "Yes."

DeeAnne looked me up and down with distaste, as if I were the cause of all their problems. "Where do we put her now?"

"It has to be downstairs," Lydia replied, "until I figure things out."

"I could rig this whole place." Max had come inside, and he rubbed the cold from his hands as he spoke. "Make it all go boom." He set his hands close together and then expanded them to simulate an explosion. "It'll be weeks before anybody figures out what happened."

Betty's eyes widened. "You're going to blow up the mill?"

"Of course not," Lydia said, shooting Max a look of warning.

"I hope not. My cats would be very frightened."

"Betty's right," DeeAnne said, but her tone told me she was placating her older sister rather than chiding the younger one.

Betty looked like she might cry. "You did say we'll take the kitty-cats with us when we go."

"Of course we will." Lydia sounded like third-grade teachers I've known, patient but not about to swerve from the lesson plan. "We haven't decided everything yet, but you know I'll take care of you."

DeeAnne put an arm around Betty. "We know that, don't we Bet?"

Betty's voice turned dreamy. "When we were little, we always took care of you. Now you've turned it all around." Her brow puckered. "But I don't like the idea of blowing up the mill, Lydia. I really don't."

"It was just an idea." I heard the lie in her voice, but Betty looked relieved.

"And we'll take the cats to Arizona. Out there, they can lie around in the sun all day." Betty seemed to picture the scene.

"Yes. Now Max and I will put Ms. Stirnum away for the night."

"Stilson," I corrected, but Lydia didn't appear to notice.

Taking my arm, Max led me down the inside stairs, and Lydia and her gun followed. "We can put them at the other end of the storeroom," he suggested. "No window on that end."

"Good idea. I'll get the man." While Max guarded me, Lydia fetched Lars. Once he and I were inside the smaller storage area, Max put the padlock in place.

"Don't talk about blowing up the mill in front of your aunts, Max. It makes them nervous."

"But I get to do it, right?"

She regarded Lars and me with a detached air. "An explosion is the best solution for these two. I'm just not sure where we should do it."

"What do you mean?"

"Max, anything that happens on our property will focus attention on us. We need to slip away quietly."

"Oh."

She patted his arm. "You'll get the chance to show off your skills, son. Kye's working on it."

Max looked put out, and I guessed he'd been eager to destroy the mill. "You need to let me know pretty soon. I can't just blow something up with fifteen minutes' notice."

"As soon as I know, you'll know." As they went up the stairs, I thought I heard Lydia sigh. Apparently keeping all her crooks in line was a tough job.

As soon as they were gone, Lars took me into his arms, and we held each other tightly for a while. Once we were somewhat reassured, we began scouting our new prison for possible escape. He checked the padlock and tested the chain while I examined the fencing for weak spots. When we found nothing, Lars went to the freight elevator and studied it. I followed. On the sales floor the shaft was enclosed, no doubt for safety reasons. On ground level it was open on three sides for easy accessibility. Perhaps twelve feet overhead, the car rested on the main floor, blocking the shaft. "Possible," Lars muttered.

"What are you thinking?"

"When the car goes up, there's an opening onto the main floor."

I saw what he was thinking. "We can climb up there and crawl over the safety gate before the car comes back down."

"There's nothing to climb." He indicated the elevator's guide rails, two simple metal posts with nothing to grasp for an upward climb. "You could hang onto the bottom of the car, ride up with it, and transfer to the cage when you get to the opening."

"Don't you mean *we* could do that?"

"I'll need to lift you up so you can reach it."

Again he was right. "I'll find something up there to drop down to you, a rope maybe."

Lars shook his head. "No time. They always return the car to the middle floor, so the hole will only open up for a few seconds."

I stopped wasting my breath and accepted what had to happen.

"Let yourself out of the building and go for help," Lars said. When I grabbed hold of him, wishing there were some other way, he hugged me back and stroked my hair. "I'll be fine, Retta. You'll have the cops here before they even know you're gone."

I tried for a confident smile. "Okay. Let's practice, so we'll be ready when the time comes."

CHAPTER EIGHTEEN

Barb

I woke at midnight with an image of Retta's bleeding corpse that was so real I almost screamed aloud. It took a few seconds to recall where I was. Green Bay. Faye in the big bed, me on the cot, Styx in the bathtub. Neither of them stirred as I sat up, shaking my head to dispel the last of the horrible dream.

Retta isn't dead. Retta's fine—or if not fine, still savable. We just have to use our heads.

Rising, I went to the window and peeped out. The street was quiet, and everything about the view indicated cold: banks of snow piled along the parking lot. Air so clear the stars looked closer than usual. A single pedestrian hurried by, clutching her coat at the neck, her head as far into the collar as she could get it.

A sign across the street advertised *Try Our Sandwitches! Their Better Then Most!* Above it, a single plastic bag fluttered in a tree, stuck on one of its lowest branches. Both those things irritated me, perhaps more than usual at the moment. I'd given up being the Grammar Nazi from necessity, but it would help at this point in time to fix something. Besides, the argumentative part of my brain said I'd never stipulated *where* I would no longer correct abuses of the English language. This was a whole different state.

The sign was one of those with movable letters, so it wouldn't take long to fix it. With sudden urgency I pulled on my boots and stuck my pajama pants into the tops. Pulling on my coat, hat, and gloves, I took my key and slipped quietly out the door. Staying in the shadows until the last possible moment, I looked around. No one in sight. Approaching the sign,

I took the *t* out of *sandwiches*. That was the easy part. I decided to eliminate *their* entirely: the message would stand without it. That left *then,* which should be *than.* I had no *a* to replace the offending *e,* so I turned it upside down. It wasn't perfect, but it was better.

That done, I looked around again. Still no one in sight. I climbed onto the sign base, which boosted me up just high enough to relieve the poor tree of its ugly hitchhiker.

"You okay up there?" a voice said, and I almost tumbled from my perch. Looking down, I saw a teenager on the sidewalk, one earbud in, one out. He wore a hoodie with a fleece vest over it, jeans, and boots that appeared to be three sizes too big. A black backpack was slung over his shoulder, and a chain that I assumed was attached to his belt hung down to his knees. The cord for the earbuds disappeared into the jacket. His hands were hidden in the side pockets, and one of them bulged with something more than a hand. I imagined a weapon: a knife? A bludgeon? A gun?

Aware of my awkward position, I climbed down and met him face to face. His expression said he hadn't yet decided what to think of me. "You shouldn't be out here alone in the middle of the night."

It sounded like a threat. As coolly as I could manage, I said, "You are."

He dragged a knuckle across his nose. "I can take care of myself."

The implication was that I couldn't, and I waited for him to demand my money. I considered my options. I could run, but fifty-four probably wouldn't beat seventeen. I could tell him I had no money with me, but he probably wouldn't believe that. I could try to act tough, but just looking at him, I knew he was tougher.

Or I could tell the truth. "I came out to fix the sign. It had a bunch of things misspelled, and I hate that."

His face, at least the half I could see in the light of a streetlamp, showed disbelief. "You're out at midnight correcting spelling?"

I raised my hands in a gesture of helplessness. "Things bug me. I fix what I can and try to ignore the rest."

"You do this stuff all the time?"

"I used to."

Suddenly white teeth flashed in a smile that lit the night. "Damn! That's kewl!" Pulling a can of spray paint from his pocket, he held it out for me to see. "I'm a graff slut too!"

In my head I translated the term from context. He saw me as a fellow graffiti artist, though that wasn't how I saw myself. I didn't vandalize buildings or train cars. I certainly didn't tag my work.

The kid pointed over his shoulder. "I just did a piece down there. Turned this ugly old shed into a rembrandt." As he moved, I heard the metallic clink of spray paint cans in the backpack.

I searched my mind for a word, but the best I could manage was "Awesome."

He took a step back and regarded me. "How long you been a writer— like thirty years, I bet."

Was there any sense telling him that his kind of "writer" and I were completely different? Probably not. "Um, no. I only started a couple of years ago."

I'd begun revising my original impression of the kid. He'd scared me at first, but that was because it was midnight in a strange area. He seemed eager to talk. His English showed that he had a decent education. He didn't feel like a threat as we conversed on a subject we both felt strongly about but couldn't discuss with others.

The difference in my mind was that I did what I did for the good of the world while he defaced property. "What makes you want to spray-paint other people's buildings?"

He took a moment to decide if I really wanted to know the answer. "First, I'm good at it, so it makes me feel, you know, kind of proud."

I could relate to that. My command of the language led me to notice the mistakes of others. I fixed them, even when the people who'd made those mistakes didn't care and even objected to my intervention.

"Second," he went on, "I make things better. Some ugly metal box or run-down brick wall—I turn it into art."

I understood that too. While I didn't create beauty as such, I created order, which for me was just as good.

"And I make other people feel better," he said. "Not the dudes who run the city or the cops that get in the way of most kinds of fun, but my people. They don't have money to go to museums or travel to Europe or even buy pretty pictures to hang on the wall at home. They start off for work or school some morning, and there it is: something new and bright and cheerful for them to look at."

Again we agreed—in a way. I had often imagined those who noticed my corrections and thought, "Good! Someone fixed that ghastly error!"

Still, his graffiti habit could land the kid in big trouble. Seizing a possible teaching moment. I said, "I almost got caught a month or so ago, and I realized how bad that would be."

The ghost of a smile lit his face. "When you really care about something, the thought of getting in trouble for it doesn't stop you."

"But it would embarrass your family, and people would see you in a completely different way."

He tilted his head to one side. "So what other people think should influence your idea of what's right and what's wrong?"

"Well, yes and no. I wouldn't like being—" I stopped. What was it I feared? Ridicule? Criminal charges? What were my standards worth?

This young man must see me as a poser, someone who believed in a cause but was unwilling to risk the repercussions of standing up for it. As we stood silent for a few seconds, I imagined his scorn for me. One scare and I'd quit. With so many corrections still to make, I'd given up. Instead of saying, "I'll be more careful" or "I don't care what happens," I'd given up. The kid probably thought my campaign was dumb anyway. He created art; I corrected billboards.

Then he said, "Know what I hate? When people mix up *too* and *to*." Pointing at me, he backed away. "You should keep up the good work."

"Good luck to you." Stuffing the bag in my pocket, I went back to the motel. After listening for a moment I let myself in, closing the door quickly in order to minimize the draft. Faye didn't wake up, and even more surprisingly, neither did Styx. Tossing the plastic bag into the garbage can, I looked at the view. It was much improved—for about twenty seconds. As I watched, helpless to stop it, the driver of a passing car tossed a drink cup out the window. It rolled to the curb and lay there, taunting me.

109

I can't correct all the mistakes. I can't clean up all the litter. And right now, I can't think of a single thing I can do to save my sister.

CHAPTER NINETEEN

Faye

When I checked my phone Tuesday morning, I found a rambling message from my sister-in-law Wanda, filled with inaccuracies and spelling errors.

> *Faye you need to talk this over with dale becuz were going ahead with a lawyer and that. Mom never ment to cheat her kids out of their inhertance, and were going to fix it. Im not saying dale did anything rong, but somebody shoud of kept her from leaving everything to that church. Churchs ain't even taxed like the rest of us are and thats not write. I called one of the lawyers that adv on tv and he sas hell look into it so you guys better talk and get in on this or get left behind. If we split the lawyer fee five ways it will be cheeper then four.*

Gritting my teeth, I wrote a quick response. *I'm out of state on business. I will mention this to Dale but I doubt he'll be interested.*

Then I erased Wanda's message. Heaven forbid Barb should see that mess. She had enough to stress about.

CHAPTER TWENTY

Retta

It was nerve-wracking to stand in the elevator shaft, waiting for the moment the cage would start up. Lars' watch had broken when he fell, and I always use my phone to check the time, so we didn't know if it was nine p.m. or midnight. We practiced a few times, Lars lifting me up until I could reach the bottom of the car. There weren't any easy handholds, and it didn't help that the temperature was less than fifty-five degrees. I tried wearing my gloves, but they were too slippery. I stuffed them into my pocket just as the elevator motor engaged, scaring me half to death.

"Is it time?"

"Let's do it." Lars put his hands on his knees, and I climbed onto his shoulders. Slowly he stood, raising me to the point where I could reach the lip of the elevator base. Whoever was above me was slow about getting into the car, which was good. Once I found the gripping places I'd chosen during practice, I pulled one foot up and wedged my boot-heel into the lip at the base of the car. I felt a sense of loss as Lars let go of my ankles, but it was comforting to know he was down there, ready to catch me if I fell.

Just as the car started moving, I braced my other foot at the opposite side, distributing my weight as evenly as possible. Every muscle involved protested the task of supporting the unusual position, but I told myself it was only twelve seconds, much shorter than the planks I do every morning.

The slow ascent gave me time to imagine what came next. I might lose a hand- or foot-hold and fall. I might misjudge the dismount and crash into the cage, above or below the exit. I might make such a noisy landing that the rider would hear and come back down to investigate.

When I could see sales area, I realized we'd made a mistake. Three figures stood with their backs to me. Lydia sorted through documents, handed some to DeeAnne, who passed them on to Max, who tossed them into the wood stove. The Whites were covering their tracks, and if one of them happened to turn and look at the elevator, I'd soon be in full view, hanging there like a monkey. I couldn't continue up. I was afraid to drop down. I had to get out of sight.

Reaching out, I grabbed a bar of the cage with one hand and another with the other. I released my feet, and there was a muted clunk as my body hit the grid. Since the machinery was noisy, none of them noticed. Cautiously I slid down the bars of the cage until all that was visible to anyone who looked my way were my hands and the top of my head. As the car continued up I hung in the shaft, breathless from both fear and exertion. The shifting of papers from hand to hand continued, and the fire glowed hot with sheet after sheet for fuel.

What should I do? The car would come back down soon, so I couldn't stay where I was. There was nothing below me but air, and my feet dangled too far overhead for Lars to reach. Should I drop and hope he could catch me? A change in sound told me the mechanism had reversed direction. Whatever I was going to do, it had to happen quickly.

I shouldn't have worried. Lars whispered, "Let go!" and grasped my feet. I did as he said, and he slowly lowered his hands. I let go of the cage, teetering ungracefully, as Lars lowered my feet to his shoulders. From there I slid to the ground as the car thudded into place overhead.

Lars held onto my shoulders until I got control of my nerves and muscles again. "Max, DeeAnne, and Lydia are up there, burning documents," I told him.

"They sent Betty up to bed. I hope the other two take the elevator when they go up."

"I think we can count on DeeAnne."

"They're leaving soon, but I think they're waiting for something."

"A sale?"

Probably. I heard them mention something that will happen on Thursday."

"So we're okay until then?"

"I wouldn't go that far, but it's easier to move live prisoners around than it is dead bodies."

The safety gate unlatched above us. "Ready to try it again?"

We hurried into place, and again I took the best hold I could manage. This time as the car's rise brought me level with the showroom, everything was dark. I reached out, grabbed the door frame, and transferred my weight to the cage. The safety gate opened almost silently, and I swung into the room with only the smallest of boot-heel clicks upon landing. As the car stopped at the top with its usual clunk, I brushed grease from my hands onto my pants, which were ruined anyway. Soon it rattled its way back down, and I looked up to make sure it was empty. Once it settled, the sales floor went quiet, but I stood still for a few minutes listening to the sisters' footsteps above. As my eyes adjusted, I saw a few faint lights nearby: the green of a computer power strip and the softer light of some glow-in-the-dark items in the front window that had picked up a bit of a charge.

I tiptoed silently down an aisle toward those lights. It was spooky, since dark forms loomed over me all the way along, but in my head I repeated what Mom used to tell us: *There's nothing in the dark that wasn't there in the light.* Pressing my lips together so hard it hurt, I reached the front door.

It wouldn't open.

After a moment my fingers found the reason: a metal bar that extended across both doors and dropped into a slot. I wasted some time trying to pull it free, but I guessed that either a key was required or the press of a switch I couldn't see. I jerked at it, frustrated. How was I going to get out?

Then I remembered the back door, where we'd come in after Max caught me. Retracing my steps, I made my way along the narrow aisle for a few feet and then stopped. Someone was playing a game of some sort only inches away from me.

I tried to picture where I was in the store. There'd been some end tables with lamps, an old sewing machine, and a fainting couch. The sounds came from there, which made sense. Max had made himself a bed in the store, probably to be handy when needed.

I waited a full twenty minutes, hardly daring to breathe. The phone went dark about halfway through that time, and I heard Max settling in on the couch, some rustling, a belch, and a long sigh. I waited until his breathing was deep and regular before, moving with agonizing caution, I sidled past the couch. A few feet away the aisle opened onto the passageway along the counter, and I put a hand on its edge to guide myself around it. Just a few feet to the exit. *Walk slowly. Set your heels down quietly. Don't breathe out loud.*

Here's a question: Don't cats curl up with their tails wrapped neatly around their bodies? If that's the case, why did I have to encounter the only cat in the world who apparently slept with its tail extended?

I knew I stepped on something. Screaming like a B movie actress, the cat ran under the counter. Before I could recover from the scare, a hand snaked into my hair and pulled me backward. "Damn, lady," Max said. "You sure are hard to keep in one place."

CHAPTER TWENTY-ONE

Barb

I called the city police Tuesday morning and spoke with the officer in charge of looking into the disappearances of Lars and Retta. "I visited the shop you told me about and interviewed the lady there," he said. "She's got no idea where your friends went."

"They each went to that place and never came back. Isn't that suspicious?"

His tone was patient. "And you have an explanation in both cases. You don't like it, but there it is." As a stranger from out-of-state, I should have known better than to question a citizen's honesty without incontrovertible proof.

"My sister left her dog behind. She wouldn't do that voluntarily."

"She knew you'd take care of it, didn't she?" When I didn't answer he went on, "This isn't the first time I've seen a woman choose a boyfriend over what her family thinks she should do. You need to give her some time."

Without local help to resolve our doubts about the White sisters, Faye and I decided to pay Critterz another visit. We found the shop door locked and a sign that said, *Experiencing Electrical Outage-Sorry for the Inconvenience*. In the window two cats slept peacefully, catching a slit of sunlight the porch roof didn't block.

Faye led the way around to the back, where she knocked on a second door for some time with no result. Finally she climbed the outside staircase and pounded on that door. Nothing. Rejoining me, she sighed in frustration. "Let's find someone who knows them. Maybe they have a reputation for cheating people or irritating their neighbors."

They didn't. We drove in a circle, stopping at businesses and engaging clerks and proprietors in conversation, bringing it around to the White sisters in various ways. No one had a bad word to say about them, though everyone admitted they kept to themselves a lot, so it was hard to judge.

"I get them mixed up," a man at the local Walgreen's told us. "Is DeeAnne the little one that dresses like Lady Gaga?"

"That's her."

He nodded. "She comes in sometimes for makeup and stuff. Seems really nice."

A woman at a local copy shop had a similar impression of Betty. "She's so sweet. Always on about the Packers or her cats."

There was a little less warmth when Lydia's name came up, but she was the bill-payer in the business, and her prompt attention to that led to approval, if not approbation.

Everyone we talked to mentioned cats. Apparently they talked a lot about theirs, so people they traded with often knew the cats' names, even if they'd never been to the store.

"They sure don't sound like crooks," Faye said when we'd visited half a dozen places and received similar responses.

"Someone there is dealing in stolen goods," I muttered. "It's time we found out more about Lydia's grandchildren."

Faye nodded. "Back to the computer?"

"First let's re-visit the mall and see if anyone's home."

There were no cars in the front parking lot, but at the back there were three: a PT Cruiser I guessed belonged to the sisters, a flatbed truck they probably used for transporting goods, and, at the other end of the building, a Honda with a bike rack.

"That could belong to one of the other vendors," I told Faye. "I'll see if I can get him or her to talk to me."

"I'll look up Kylie and Max on my phone," Faye said, "though I make no promises without a full-size screen."

I parked at the front of the building and left the engine running to keep Faye warm. Climbing the stairs, I picked up a couple of bits of plastic tossed carelessly away and deposited them in the trash before looking in the windows of the other businesses. There was no sign of life inside the sports memorabilia shop, nor in the used books and records place. I stopped when I saw movement inside the craft store. A woman was sorting squares of fabric into piles. A quilter. I rapped at the door and indicated with gestures that I wanted to speak with her.

She was fortyish and plain, with wide blue eyes and a nice smile. "I'm not open—" she began, but I put up a hand.

"I'm not here to shop. I'm looking into the disappearance of a friend of mine."

A frown creased her forehead. "The guy the cops were looking for? I thought they found him."

"Not yet, at least not in the flesh. There was a message, but it might be fake."

Her eyes widened. "Oh, my."

119

"I'm wondering if you can tell me about the people at Critterz."

"Oh, the White sisters! So cute! I mean they're all so different, but they get along well." The frown returned momentarily. "I guess they disagree sometimes, but sisters always argue, don't they?"

I agreed enthusiastically, pleased to have found a natural gossip. "I've met the sisters, but I'm wondering if there's someone else to help with moving things and such."

"Well, sure, there's Max. He seems a little weird at first, but he's okay, and he can fix just about anything. He sharpens my scissors, and once I had this quilt stretcher that came in about a hundred pieces, and he put it all together for me. I mean, I always pay him. Max doesn't have a real job so he does what he can in the way of odd jobs and then he helps out at the store."

"Why doesn't he have a job, do you know?"

She pressed her lips together as if telling herself it wasn't nice to gossip. In the end the desire to share was stronger than her reserve. "I think he was in jail."

"I see."

"But he isn't a bad guy. Somebody probably said, 'It would be fun to steal this car,' so he did. If something gets him an atta-boy, Max will do it."

He didn't sound like a criminal mastermind, but I asked, "Where does Max live?"

"I'm not sure. I think he's gone a lot, picking up or delivering. Sometimes I see him out there smoking early in the morning, so I guess he stays here sometimes." A thought came to her. "I think they have another place. I've heard Betty mention storing stuff at the farm."

"Is anyone else involved in the business?"

"Well, Kye, of course, but she isn't around much. She's like their buyer, so she travels all over looking for stuff they can sell."

"What's she like?"

Again her conscience battled the desire to tell. "She's gorgeous, and they're always telling how smart she is, but I can't say I've ever gotten to know her. She doesn't share much."

"Is she in Green Bay now?"

She shrugged. "Last I knew she was in California. I guess she does like those two guys on TV, goes around buying up people's old stuff."

"Did you ever have a sense any of the Whites were hiding something? Any suspicious customers or clandestine activity?"

I'd gone too far. "I don't spy on my landlords," she said primly. "And I don't gossip about them to strangers."

I could have pointed out she'd been doing exactly that, but instead I thanked her and went back to the car, where Faye had new information. "No convictions for DeeAnne's son Roddy, though he was arrested in 2003. He peed on one of the lions outside the New York Public Library, for reasons that aren't clear but might involve alcohol."

"Charming."

She gave me half a smile. "Lydia's grandkids are of more interest. They were arrested for burglary in 2011 when a safe in the bar where Kylie worked was blown open with a crude explosive." She tilted her head at me. "And I quote grandson Max Hayworth: 'It made a lot bigger noise than I expected.' Max was caught on site, convicted of several crimes, and served two years. Kylie apparently had a better lawyer. She went into the military in lieu of being charged as an accessory."

"Lucky girl," I commented.

"Especially since she was probably the brains behind the break-in. Max is no genius. Prison records indicate he's almost a non-reader, though he does have a talent for mechanics and such."

"How did the girl do in the military?"

"Very well in areas like weaponry. Not so well in conduct, though she usually avoided serious punishment. Here's why, in my opinion." Turning the tablet my way, she showed me two photos. Kylie (a.k.a. Kye, according to her rap sheet) was gorgeous, with long, dark hair and bright eyes. Though her face was serious in the military photo, a shot from high school revealed a smile that I figured turned men's hearts into little blobs of Jell-O.

Faye touched the screen a few times. "Here's big brother." Max had gotten the short end of the gene pool as far as physical beauty went, with a rodent-like face, greasy complexion, and lank hair. He wasn't smiling in his mug shot, but I pictured sharp little teeth beneath those thin lips. "That's the guy who was outside smoking when you asked that shop owner about Lars."

She turned the phone back. "You're right. And soon after we got a call that sent us to Manitowoc on a wild goose chase."

I pulled my gloves off and tossed them on the dashboard. "Think the younger generation could be using their elderly relatives as a front for selling stolen goods?"

"That's more likely than Betty White, ultimate Packer-Backer, peddling contraband. But why kidnap Lars? Why not just run?"

"They sent Retta that text to explain Lars' absence. They made her call us to explain hers. They're trying to delay a possible investigation, probably to give themselves time for a getaway."

"If that's true," Faye said, "they'll release Lars and Retta when whatever they're waiting for is done."

"Probably." I tried to make my tone bright, but in criminal plots, when things go wrong, crooks panic. And when they panic, they cut their losses. *Then* they run.

CHAPTER TWENTY-TWO

Faye

Agent Stiles was waiting for us when we got back to the motel. "Where have you been, ladies?"

"Shopping," Barb said breezily. "Faye thought as long as we were in Wisconsin, she might as well pick up Packer stuff for her grandkids."

She turned to me. "What did you buy?"

As I hesitated, unwilling to lie, Barb said, "We didn't find just the thing, but we heard there's a cheese shop north of here, near Oconto. We'll stop there on the way home, once we know Retta is okay."

Now, Barb isn't a great liar either, but she managed to deflect without deceiving. There might well be a great cheese shop in Oconto. We just had no idea if there was or where it might be.

Stiles dropped the subject. "Have you heard from your sister again?"

"No." We spoke together, but Barb went on. "But we do have a question for you. Are you working with a partner?"

Her eyes tightened. "No. Why do you ask?"

"We heard through the grapevine about a man asking questions at the store. He told them he might go to the police with information he has about Lydia's granddaughter."

That made Stiles take note. "Which grapevine did you hear it on?"

Barb put on her best lawyer manner. "I'm afraid I can't reveal the source of the information."

She rolled her eyes. "What can you tell me about this man?"

"Medium height and build, mid-thirties, dark hair done up in a knot, lots of white teeth, big voice."

That interested her. "Sounds like you saw him."

"What difference does it make?"

Stiles sighed. "I'm trying to keep you ladies safe. I'll look into this, but you need to stop interfering. Please."

"I'm sure you're very capable." Again Barb didn't lie, but she didn't say we'd stop looking for Retta either. Why would we sit on our hands when our sister was in trouble?

When Stiles left I checked my phone, which had signaled several text messages. All were from Wanda. All claimed it was "critacal" we talk. I deleted them and went back to trying to find out more about Critterz helper Max and the elusive Kylie, who didn't seem to live anywhere.

CHAPTER TWENTY-THREE

Retta

My third place of imprisonment was the bathroom, which had a sturdy door and no other means of exit. Its worst attribute, other than being grimy and the size of a checkerboard, was distance from Lars. With space and walls between us, I doubted he'd hear me even if I shouted.

"Same arrangement as before," Lydia told me. "If you behave, I let Betty feed you. Give us grief and you can rot in here for all I care." With that she closed the door on me and I discovered another drawback: she'd taken the light bulb from its socket.

Sometime in the early morning hours, DeeAnne brought breakfast, wearing palazzo pants and a shirt that brought to mind a James Bond girl, maybe Jill St. John. On a china tray were toast with jam and a cup of black coffee. It wasn't my usual preference, but I was ready to down anything that smelled vaguely of coffee beans. Setting the tray on the chipped enamel sink, she stepped back. "Max is at the top of the stairs," she said. "You won't get by him, even if you attack me."

"I'm not going to attack you, DeeAnne. I just don't think you understand the trouble you're in."

She waved my warning away with a dramatic gesture, but then, all of DeeAnne's gestures were dramatic. "We'll be long gone before anyone finds out you're here. We'll tell the police you're down here, so you won't starve or anything."

"You really think Lydia's going to just let us go?"

"Why not? Once we get our money, you'll be of no further use."

"Money?"

Her eyes lit with greed. DeeAnne might not understand the implications of what they were doing, but she approved wholeheartedly of the possible rewards. "We're coming into a nice little pot of gold. No more wasting away in this place and no frigid winters. We'll live out our days in comfort and style." She added as a sop, "You and your boyfriend will be fine, but they'll never find us. Lydia and Kye have it worked out so we just disappear." She made an abracadabra gesture.

Did she really not get that Lars and I weren't going to be fine, or didn't it matter as long as she had the life she'd always wanted? Even if Barbara Ann and Faye screamed for an investigation, who'd believe three apparently harmless women sold illegal goods, kidnapped innocent people, and committed murder? Especially if an explosion obliterated the evidence.

When Betty brought my lunch a few hours later, I tried again. She seemed the most approachable of the three, kinder than Lydia—not that almost everyone wasn't—and less self-absorbed than DeeAnne. "How long have you lived at the Old Mill?" I asked as she handed me a plate with a roast beef sandwich and a homemade dill pickle.

"Almost ten years," she said. "We own a house in the country— that's where we grew up, and I lived out there for a long time." She gestured around us. "This was my uncle's mill, and I worked for him, so when he died, he left it to me."

"And you turned it into an antique mall."

"I opened the shop on this end, but Lydia came up with the idea of renting space to other businesses and moving in upstairs." Her eyes got dreamy again. "I miss the farm sometimes, but here I can walk to

Lambeau Field anytime I want. Sometimes I just wait in the parking lot and watch the Packers going in to practice."

"All three of you stayed in Green Bay?"

"Oh, no! DeeAnne was an actress, who traveled all over. She was so beautiful playing Cleopatra or Tatiana!" She clasped her hands. "Not that I ever saw her on stage, but she shows me pictures. When she retired, she came to live with Lydia and me."

"And what did Lydia do for a living?"

Betty's brows got closer together. "Something in the import-export business out in Pennsylvania. But then her daughter died, so she brought her grandchildren here. We all lived out at the farm until the kids graduated, then we moved in here to save the expense of keeping up two places." Her expression turned wistful. "I miss the farm sometimes, but it was a bear to keep up in the wintertime." She returned to her story. "Anyway, Lydia took over the business, and I helped with the kids." After pressing her lips together for a moment she added, "She's made more money than I could ever have."

I figured Lydia had been a criminal in her former life, possibly a fence in some larger organization where she'd learned the ropes of handling stolen goods. Forced to return to Green Bay, she'd enlisted her slightly dim sister's help as a laundress, cook, and general babysitter while she turned Betty's little business into a network for contraband.

"What about the grand-daughter? Where is she?"

Betty's eyes softened. "Kye's our buyer now that it's hard for us to get around like we used to."

So Kylie—Kye—was Nana Lydia's second-in-command, with Max as all-around henchman.

"Betty, you know the goods you sell are stolen, right?"

"Not all of them, dear." She bent to pick up a cat that had followed her downstairs. "We resell a few things that bad people stole years ago. They can't be returned to the rightful owners because nobody knows who they are." Leaning in she confided, "We give a share of the proceeds to the Humane Society, so kitties get healthy and find new homes."

Not likely, I thought, but I didn't argue. "I assume Lydia and Kylie are the only ones who are supposed to handle those goods."

She frowned again. "Yes. Lydia was mad at me for putting that jewelry out on Friday, but I wanted a nice display for Valentine's next month, and—" She waved helplessly.

"You got the goods mixed up, which meant my friend Lars saw what he shouldn't have seen."

"Yes." Her expression turned from concerned to pleased. "But DeeAnne called Lydia, and they handled everything."

"She hit him with a club, Betty. She might have killed him."

That possibility was dismissed with a smile. "No, Lydia knows exactly where to strike."

It was my turn to frown. "She's hit people with a club before?"

Betty set the cat down, and it wandered away. "Not people. But she worked at a meat packing company when she was in high school." She raised a fist to demonstrate. "She learned how to—"

"Please." I interrupted. "I don't need to know." I handed her the plate, though there was half a sandwich left. My appetite had suddenly disappeared.

"We always took care of her, DeeAnne and I," Betty said in the same dreamy tone I'd noticed earlier. "Now Lydia takes care of us."

It sounded like the chant of a cult member, conditioned to accept what she's told and question nothing.

CHAPTER TWENTY-FOUR

Barb

If I had to list my ten least favorite pastimes, walking Styx would be in there along with committee meetings and root canals, but dogs, unlike cats, require walking. Styx isn't fun to walk because he's so strong. A glimpse of a squirrel, the scent of a porcupine, and he's off. You can either let go of the leash or speed along behind like Wile E. Coyote attached to a rocket. I find myself praying for no wildlife sightings.

The day had been cold, and Green Bay, like Allport, sits along a very large body of water, so wind is often a factor. Still, it wasn't fair to make Faye always be the dog-sitter, so Styx and I left the motel at dusk and visited the park. The upside was that the walk was brisk; Styx is not one to dally. The downside was a cat crossing our path, for reasons I'll never understand. Cats are usually smarter than that.

Styx lunged, but luckily I saw the creature first and grabbed a convenient lamppost. I survived the initial jerk, and Styx stopped short, coughed, and let the leash slacken for a second. Quickly I wrapped it around the post twice. That might sound cruel, but it saved at least one of the cat's nine lives. Once it scurried out of sight, Styx trotted at my side as sedately as Mary's Little Lamb.

Back at the motel, I tried the FBI office in Albuquerque again. The time difference meant that it was just after four there. Like Retta, I'd gotten the runaround on my first try, so this time I said, "This is Barbara Evans of the Pierce County District Attorney's office in Tacoma, Washington. I need to speak to an agent who has worked with Lars Johannsen in the past."

Yes, I lied. But I *was* an A.D.A. in Tacoma for decades, and receptionist-type people respond better to titles than they do to unknown citizens. "One moment."

I was connected to an Agent Graves, who was cautious. "I wasn't aware Agent Johannsen had ever been to the state of Washington."

"He hasn't. The truth is, Lars and my sister Margaretta might be missing, and I wanted to speak with someone who knows him well enough to understand that the situation is suspicious."

"Margar—you mean Retta? She's your sister?"

"She is."

"She and Lars invited me and my wife over last fall when she was in town. She's quite a girl, that Retta."

"She is," I agreed. "She called me because Lars disappeared on their trip to Albuquerque."

"Where exactly?"

"Green Bay, Wisconsin." I explained their itinerary and Lars' failure to return to the motel.

"Okay." I could tell he was writing things down, which was good.

"There was an explanation by text, supposedly from Lars, but Retta didn't believe it. She called us—her other sister and me—and we came to Wisconsin to help her find him. Now Retta has disappeared, and again there's an explanation, but it's not believable if you know her."

"Tell me everything you can about what they did in Green Bay."

I went through the whole thing, with Graves interrupting from time to time to ask a question. Again, that gave the sense he was taking me seriously. When I got to the part where an FBI agent showed up at our door he asked, "Name?"

"Stiles. I looked up the local office, and a Jamie Stiles is listed as working there."

"Okay. Go on."

When I'd told him everything I could think of and he'd pulled out a few details I hadn't thought to include, Graves said, "Ms. Evans, I agree that just walking away doesn't seem like what I know of Lars. And what man would dump Retta?"

It sounded like Graves had a little crush on my sister, but that wasn't unusual. "We'll appreciate anything you can do."

He called back in less than an hour. "We've had no word from Lars the last few days, but he did check the stolen goods database. I've sent you screenshots of the items he looked at."

"Is one of them a ring?"

"Yes. The pieces he looked at were once part of the National Museum of Iraq."

"Valuable stuff?"

"Some of it was. Some was just old. Looters took whatever they could get their hands on."

"And unloaded it in Green Bay, Wisconsin?"

Graves chuckled. "It's possible. Some contractor or deployed soldier buys the stuff and brings it home. Ten, fifteen years later, the guy's heirs have no clue what they've got. They sell it to some dealer, and nobody knows where it goes from there. Maybe Green Bay."

"It's terrible," I said. "Millennia of artifacts gone forever."

"Actually, we have a pretty good record of recovery," Graves objected. "Agent Stiles will track the stuff down, and whoever has it will have to give it back."

"What's the White sisters' liability?"

"Amateur dealers might unknowingly buy a stolen piece or two, but if they have bunches, we'd look at them pretty hard."

Lars had gone back to the store, at least to the parking lot outside it. Someone had seen him as a threat. The question was who? Some elderly woman whose main interest in life was football and cats?

"I phoned the Green Bay office and asked Agent Stiles to call me back," Graves said. "I'll add a little weight to the scale from my end."

"We appreciate that, Agent Graves."

"Bill," he corrected. "Call me anytime at this number." He sighed. "I'd like to come up there myself and hunt for Lars, but if you pay attention to the news, you know we've got plenty down here to keep us busy right now."

"I understand."

"Lars is a good friend. I hope he turns up safe and sound."

"Agent Graves—Bill—maybe together we can do more than hope."

CHAPTER TWENTY-FIVE

Retta

When the bathroom door opened for the third time, it was late in the day on Tuesday, to the best of my ability to calculate. Lydia was backlit by a hanging bulb behind her, holding the pistol confidently. Everything else was black.

"Come with me."

Behind her was Max, who held a bunch of zip ties. When I stepped out, he pulled my hands behind my back and fastened them there with one of them.

"Do you even care that you've put your sisters at risk of going to prison for the rest of their lives?" I asked.

Lydia's head jerked. "They've spent their lives living like paupers. Now the bills are paid. DeeAnne can buy all the gaudy clothes she wants, and Betty can feed her cats organic, tummy-safe food instead of dollar store crap. They're ten times better off than they were."

"And what about the people you cheat?"

"If you buy stolen goods, you deserve whatever happens to you. I'm not to blame for someone else's greed."

I was pushed and prodded toward the steps and out the back door, where the delivery truck waited, its bed draped with a tarp and its engine running. Guessing they'd waited for the other mall vendors to go home before moving their prisoners, I decided it was probably between six and eight p.m.

Max helped me climb onto the flatbed and held up the cover as I crawled under it. Following at a crouch, he fastened a second zip tie around my ankles. With a third he bound my hands to an upright pole near the cab. I wouldn't be able to roll off as the truck went down the road, even if that seemed like a good idea. Last he duct-taped my mouth, which felt horrible. I must have looked terrified, because he said almost kindly, "It's just to keep you quiet till we get there."

A few minutes later the process was repeated with Lars, who shot me a look but said nothing. When he was secured and gagged, Max got in up front, ground the shifter into first, and through a small gap in the tarp we watched Lydia get smaller and smaller as we rode away.

The ride wasn't all that long, but it was definitely uncomfortable. My arms ached from their unusual position, and even though I kept scooting my rear toward the cab, the bouncing of the truck shook me in the opposite direction. I'd never thought of myself as a mouth breather, but it was difficult having only my nose for taking in air. The tie around my ankles was so tight it cut into the skin. From muted groans beside me, I knew Lars was as miserable as I was.

We made a succession of turns, leaving the lights of Green Bay behind on roads that got progressively narrower and less traveled. The truck finally slowed, made a left turn, went down a bumpy but blessedly short driveway, and stopped. We had arrived at the place where they intended to kill us.

Max jumped onto the truck bed, a flashlight in one hand and a jackknife in the other, and cut first the tie at my ankles and then the one that held me to the pole. "Come on," he ordered, and I scooted along the rough planks until my feet hung over the edge. He helped me down, supporting me until my numb legs were able to hold me upright.

136

Darkness and quiet surrounded us, the only illumination a halogen light mounted on a twenty-foot pole at the center of the space. A single lamp glowed softly inside a farmhouse I guessed was the one Betty had told me about. The White family farm. Clapboard-sided and stark, the house was two-and-a-half stories without a single decorative touch: no porch, no shutters, and only a narrow set of steps at the entry. A trapdoor along one wall probably led either to an unfinished basement or a root cellar. Near it sat a four-wheeler, an older model from the look of it. The house brought to mind several horror movies I'd seen. I couldn't help but peek to see if a guy with an axe was sneaking up behind me.

Nothing moved in the bluish glow of the outside light. I took a step toward the house, but Max took my arm and turned me. "You're sleeping there." Set into a hillside, the barn was a cinder-block rectangle with an arched-roof hayloft atop it. A regular sized door in the near end was for human use, and a wider one in the center of the front wall, meant for cattle to pass in and out, was closed and padlocked. When Max opened the smaller door and gestured me inside, I saw nothing but darkness, but I smelled hay, animal sweat, and manure. "Go in," he urged, gesturing me inside. Shooting him a glare I obeyed. At the last moment I thought of a favor he might grant.

"Will you cut my hands free? I have to pee, and they're numb."

He thought about it then took out his jackknife and cut the zip-tie with one swift motion. As I rubbed my hands to get the circulation going again, he backed away, and a second later the door closed and a hasp clicked into place outside, locking me in. Max's voice came through the planks, muffled. "Make a nest in the hay and you'll stay warm. I got to see to your friend the FBI man."

The place was cold, though not freezing, and some low sounds to my left told me why. I had cows for companions, four of them. That was good, because their body heat would keep me warm—well, somewhat warm. Zipping my coat, I reached into my pockets for my gloves. They weren't there, and I realized they'd probably fallen out while I hung in the elevator shaft at the old mill. Disgusted, I buried my hands in my coat-sleeves and moved to one of the barn's two windows. Where would Max put Lars? Not with me, since together we'd almost escaped their clutches twice.

The windows were covered with chicken wire, probably to keep rats, mice, and other small creatures out. The glass was filthy, but I rubbed a spot clean with my sleeve in order to watch Max. He didn't return to the truck but went into the house. In only a few seconds he came back outside with an attractive woman whose posture clearly revealed irritation. Because the night air was crisp, I heard every word as if they were standing next to me. "It's friggin' cold out!" she said, pulling on a coat as she followed Max. Taking a hat from the pocket, she jammed it over her dark hair.

"Gram said not to try to handle him alone," Max replied. "He's so big it looks like he ate his brother."

"Why didn't you bring the gun?"

"She don't want me touching it. Just stand by with the tire iron, so he don't get ideas." He held out his makeshift weapon.

Before taking it the woman fished mittens out of her pockets and put them on. "All right. Get him off of there."

I lost sight of them when they went to the truck, so the rest I only heard. First they threatened Lars: If he tried to escape he'd not only get beaned with the metal bar but also get me killed. Max helped him off the truck and directed him to the house, where I heard the creak of doors opening. "Down there," Max ordered. A few seconds later, I heard a double slam. They'd put Lars in the root cellar, a hole in the ground with only one way in or out. Next I heard the four-wheeler start up, go a short distance, and stop. "Let him try to move that!" Max said, and his sister— it had to be Kylie—chuckled. They'd parked the ATV atop the root cellar's flat doors. Even if he was able to break the latch, my poor Lars was buried, like a corpse in a tomb.

That meant getting us out of this mess was up to me.

CHAPTER TWENTY-SIX

BARB

"Say the word and I can be over there in five hours." Rory was understandably upset that Retta and Lars were missing, but he was almost as upset to hear that we'd been dismissed by the local police. He's proud of the brotherhood, and a failing of one is for him a mark on the honor of all.

"I think a phone call would be sufficient," I told him. "Just let them know our heads aren't stuffed with 'cotton, hay, and rags' as Henry Higgins would have it."

"I'll call first thing in the morning, so I reach someone with clout."

His internet search had garnered responses, but nothing useful. "Mostly we're getting men who claim Retta drove by giving them come-hither glances, like Suzanne Somers in *American Graffiti.*"

I was disgusted. "Can't people just help out for once, without getting all weird?"

"People like drama," Rory responded. "If they don't have it, a lot of them manufacture it. We'll keep taking the calls. Maybe something will pan out."

I doubted anyone was going to spot Retta on the road to Albuquerque, because I was pretty sure she wasn't there.

"How are things in Allport?"

"Well, let's see. The city council is divided over whether I should reprimand young Armbruster for driving around with two huge Confederate flags flowing over his truck bed."

"These are the Armbrusters who've lived in northern Michigan since they came from Europe in the 1800s, right? How does the kid identify with the war of secession?"

"Not a question I can answer, but he has the right to be as bone-headed in public as he likes as long as he isn't breaking any laws." He turned serious. "I did hear at the county clerk's office that Dale's sister came in asking how to break a will."

"Really."

"She told them Dale had undue influence over his mother in her final years and her decisions were more his than hers."

"Anyone who knew Harriet will know that's not true."

"The clerk discouraged the idea of questioning a legally-prepared will, but she isn't sure if she got through."

"Faye usually handles that stuff. I'm not sure what Dale will do if Wanda makes trouble."

Rory cleared his throat, a sign he's saying something he feels is necessary but not likely to be popular. "You two will be home in a few days, once Retta's found. And I think Faye underestimates Dale. He's not as disabled as she assumes."

I thought about that. "He does seem more like himself lately."

"Faye should let him handle this."

"She'll have to. Right now she can't be running interference."

141

Ending the call, I spent a few seconds wondering why people get so weird when a parent dies. I'd heard all the arguments about sibling rivalries from childhood re-emerging once Mom or Dad is no longer there to referee, but it seemed to me that grownups should act like grownups. I didn't know Dale's sisters that well, but from where I stood, he was the only adult in the bunch. I hoped they didn't make too much trouble for him and Faye.

Chapter Twenty-Seven

Retta

Barbara Ann often complains that I act impulsively, so I forced myself to list the steps I would need to take so I didn't get caught a third time. First I had to get out of the barn. Then I had to free Lars. Together we'd make our way to civilization and call the police. Though it sounded simple, when people with guns and tire irons don't want you to reach your goals, those goals become a lot more difficult.

I searched the barn, mostly by touch since it was dark as the inside of a whale, as Dad used to say. Though the comparison was apt, I don't think he had a frame of reference. My groping hands and shuffling feet revealed a barn set up like many others I'd been in, two rows of stanchions, ten in each row, where cows were once fastened in place so they could be milked. Those days were long gone, and the cow quartet present at the moment rested at their ease in a corner. They didn't seem upset when I walked around. In my experience, it's hard to upset a cow.

On the outer wall hung an old milker, its stainless steel drum now dimmed by dirt and cobwebs. In the corners were assorted farm tools, most broken and not worth removing when the dairy men closed up shop.

I went to both doors and rattled, but neither offered a loose or rotten board. The hinges were on the outside, so I couldn't remove the screws and escape that way. I kicked the smaller door in anger but only ended up hurting my toe. Limping slightly, I went back around the room, skirting the outside walls in search of another exit. My eyes gradually adjusted to the ambient light, but nothing suggested a way out. A doorway at the far end led to a small tack room, but nothing there was helpful: old leather harness that was rotting away, shear-pins, rake teeth, and a can of assorted nails, screws, and bolts so rusted that the bottom stayed put when I picked it up. Leaving bits and pieces still spinning on the floor, I went back to the main room.

In our barn at home, I recalled a trapdoor between the hayloft above and the ground floor so Dad could drop bales of hay through for the cattle rather than carrying them around the exterior. I began a second search, this time looking up, and eventually detected a break of about four by four feet in the boards above me. Taking up a piece of two-by-four from a corner, I poked at the square. The trap only opened a half-inch, and I recalled ours had had a simple hook-and-eye fastener on the topside.

Since the fastener probably wasn't high tech, I might break it loose from the old wood with a few sharp taps. Picking up the board again, I began thumping at the edge opposite the hinges. At first I gave it everything I had, hoping to break the latch free. After a while I realized that light taps might be more effective, jiggling the hook out of the eye. Moving the board to one side, I hit the trapdoor gently a few times and listened. I tapped again, and then again, waiting to hear the hook fall out of place. I began to doubt myself. It might not be a hook and eye, but something more secure, like a bolt with a strike plate that would be more difficult to shake free.

Ting! The trap opened a little farther before dropping back into place. Putting my hands in a new position on the board, I pushed again, harder. It took several tries to send the door high enough that it fell open instead of slamming shut again. When it teetered then fell backward, hitting the plank floor overhead with a bang, one of the cows coughed in objection. I made a little whoop of satisfaction. I had a way out, if I could climb high enough to reach it.

I looked for something to stand on, but there wasn't much to work with. The stanchion frames, though six feet high, were anchored in place on the other side of the barn. Everything else, like a crate that looked promising for a moment, was rotten from sitting on damp concrete for ages. Staring up at where I wanted to be, I felt like that little mouse that sings "Somewhere Out There" in the movie. I could even see pale moonlight through a window at the end of the hayloft. As I bit my lip and wished, I noticed a pulley hoist directly overhead, probably thirty feet above where I stood. A rope threaded over the wheel hung tantalizingly near, perhaps only ten feet away, offering a way out if I could reach it.

I tried not to think about the bad things. Lars stuck in a hole in the ground. My sisters worried sick about us. My fingers clumsy stumps due to the cold. *Think of a way to get hold of that rope.*

I considered using a cow to boost myself up, but again, experience told me it was unlikely. Cows don't move when you want them to and move when you'd like them to be still.

I made another search of the barn, this time for something to extend my reach and catch the end of the rope. I found several items that might have been helpful but weren't: a lantern with no fuel, a hay hook with no point, and a flashlight with dead batteries (and bird poop on the handle, I realized after I'd picked it up). Then, at the back of the barn, where it was so dark I had to feel my way along, my hand touched a sturdy wooden shaft. Pulling it into better light, I saw that it was a pitchfork with one broken tine. It would extend my reach a few feet, but not quite enough.

Back to the dark tack room, where I felt around a second time. In a corner was an old gas can, empty but suitable for my purpose—sort of. The top was rounded, so it wasn't the stable footrest I'd have liked. Still, it was something. Setting the can under the hay hole, I tried to climb onto it. After my boots slid off several times, I realized I'd do better with just socks. Pulling the boots off, I tossed them up, one at a time, until they landed on the loft floor above. Using the pitchfork for balance, I stepped onto the can again and got better results. I was able to touch the wood frame but couldn't reach the top edge to pull myself through. I needed that rope.

Teetering unsteadily, I began trying to catch the knot at the end of the pulley rope between the pitchfork tines. Turning the fork to the side, I went after the knot with a swiping motion. I lost count of how many times I had it for a second, only to have it slip through and swing away. At the point where I thought my arm would fall off, I managed to twist the fork enough that the knot wedged between two tines.

Now came another tricky part: bringing the rope down to where I could grasp it. A pulley is designed to move easily both ways. If the knot slipped free, the impetus of its release might cause the rope to rise in the opposite direction, taking it out of my reach.

With great care I pulled the pitchfork down through the opening, keeping it tilted as horizontally as possible. Once it was through, I faced a new problem. Both my hands were busy: one holding the pitchfork and one keeping me balanced. If I let go of the trapdoor frame, I might slide off the gas can, probably losing the rope and possibly sustaining a pitchfork puncture upon landing. If I dropped the pitchfork, I had to grab the knot before it broke free and floated upward in that equal-and-opposite-reaction thing physics teachers love to talk about.

Turning the pitchfork tines downward as far as I could manage with one hand, I jumped off the can, working to stick my landing. When I hit, the pitchfork handle shuddered against the hard floor and the knot shook free, dancing sideways and rising toward the roof. I managed to keep my balance and reach out to catch it. "Stay here," I ordered. "I've got work to do, and you're going to help."

In possession of one end of a rope, I considered the possibilities for the invisible opposite end. If it lay loose somewhere in the hayloft, I'd be left with the whole rope coiled uselessly at my feet if I pulled too hard. It would be nice if the other end were tied off somewhere, so I could make my way up it and escape.

Of course it wasn't. When I pulled, ever so gently, on the knot, the other end glided into view overhead. As soon as I saw it I changed direction, feeding my end of the rope back up. While rope isn't easily pushed, this was the Manilla kind, thick, tightly woven, and stiff enough that I was able to reverse its path. Maneuvering patiently, I jiggled it toward me until I held both ends in my hands.

This is where the tough-guy hero (or tough-girl, in my case) would climb the rope like a circus performer and be on to the next step. I do not climb ropes, and honestly, I don't know many women over fifty who do. Slender or not, our center of gravity is at our hips, so lifting our weight with only the arms is a real challenge.

What I can do is tie a knot. I made several, each a few feet apart, in one end then end I increased the size of the original knot so it couldn't go through the pulley. I sent it up, tested it, and then used the knots as footholds, climbing to the hay-hole edge and hefting myself into the loft. That might sound easy, but possibilities for disaster loomed at every step, like the fact that a pulley that old might break or a rope that's hung in a barn for decades might snap from rot. Neither of those things happened, and I rolled onto the floor of the loft, where the large window I'd seen earlier promised freedom. All I had to do was find my boots, put them on, and go.

Except I tripped over someone about two steps along. I didn't know at first it was some*one*. I just knew some*thing* soft-ish and big caught my foot and sent me sprawling. As I hit the rough plank surface, a distinctly human word came out, one Mother would have pursed her lips at.

"Who is that?" I asked, peering into the darkness.

"You first," a low voice answered.

Though he was in the shadow of some bales, the moon lit his ankles, and I saw the zip-tie. "I'm Retta. I was a prisoner, like you." As I spoke, I looked around for a way to cut the ties. "Who are you?"

He snorted what might have been a laugh if it weren't so sad. "Right now I'd call myself Dumbass."

"What's your name?"

"Luke."

"Okay, Luke, I'm going to free you, and then you and I are going to find my friend and get away from here. Will you help me?"

"Sure." The relief in his voice was evident.

The only thing I found with an edge was an ancient sickle hanging on a nail in the wall. Its wooden handle was gone and its edge was so rusted I wasn't sure it would cut anything, but I took it back to where Luke lay and began sawing at the plastic. As I worked, he talked.

"I thought I was Kylie's boyfriend. We met in a bar and had some laughs. I invited her home, and next thing I know, she's staying at my place."

"Where do you live?"

"Madison. Anyway, she's with me for a few weeks and then one morning I wake up and she's gone. So I'm all broke up. I can't work or nothing. I mean, that girl, she can—" He thought better of finishing that sentence. "Well, she never said where she came from or nothing about herself, but I saw her contacts list once and it said *Gram*, with a Green Bay number." The tie on his legs surrendered to my sawing, and he held out his hands. "It took a while, but I tracked her down. So what does she

148

do? She ties me up like a Christmas turkey and leaves me here. I thought I was gonna freeze to death."

"Why would she do that?"

"She ain't nothing like I thought." He shook his head. "I think she killed some guy."

His words chilled me even more than the icy draft blowing through the loft. I'd held onto the hope that Betty's view of the future was possible, but if Kylie had already killed someone, the chances for others in her path to freedom weren't good.

"Why are you still alive?"

The zip tie split, and Luke rubbed at his wrists. "She said something to that guy Max about taking care of everyone all at once." He squinted at me. "Are you supposed be part of that?"

"I'm afraid so."

Kylie, Lydia, and the gang must be confounded by the number of threats to their enterprise who'd shown up lately. First Lars, then me, now this guy. Dread increased when I realized they could make a clean sweep if they added Faye and Barbara Ann to the tally.

"We need to go," I told Luke, but just then a door at the end of the room opened. Turning, I saw Kylie silhouetted in the frame. A bright light pinned us in its beam, and she ordered, "Stay where you are, both of you."

I knew better than to obey. It was dark at the sides of the barn, and our best chance of staying unharmed was if she couldn't see us. Pushing Luke ahead of me, I sprinted for a pile of hay bales on our left. We skidded to the floor behind them as a bullet whined by.

"Stay down!" I ordered softly. "When she turns the light away, we're going to jump out the window."

"Jump?" He repeated doubtfully.

"It's not that far to the ground, and the snow will cushion our fall. It will take her a minute to get out the door and around to the barnyard. With that much head start, I think we can outrun her."

After a hesitation, Luke spoke again. "I don't have to outrun her."

"What?"

"I just have to outrun you." With that he gave me a push that sent me stumbling into the light, where I sprawled onto the dusty floor.

Before I could get my breath I heard Luke's running footsteps, a pause, and then a grunt as he hit the ground below. When I looked up, Kylie stood over me with the flashlight in one hand and a gun in the other. "I've had about enough of you not staying where you're put."

I could have said I'd had enough of her and her whole family, but I was too busy spitting out bits of dirt and hay.

CHAPTER TWENTY-EIGHT

Faye

When I told Barb my idea Wednesday morning at breakfast, she shook her head. "Why didn't I think of that?"

"Warm up the car," I said, pleased with her ready agreement. "I'll get Styx ready."

He was on the bed, which he occupied whenever we didn't shoo him off. Thankfully, he didn't insist on sleeping with us, because Barb would have blown a gasket.

"Styx, do you want to go for a ride?"

I think every dog in the world understands that word. Some like it, some don't, but Styx *loves* it. I spread several towels in the back. Hosting a one-hundred-forty-pound dog would be a first for Barb's car, and she wasn't going to like it.

Styx was an angel, at least compared to other trips I'd shared with him. Usually he wants to ride in front. If you're in the passenger seat, he assumes you want him on your lap. This time he stayed in the back, though he did stick his head between us in order to see the road ahead. I wiped drool off Barb's console as unobtrusively as possible.

The sign on the Critterz door said it was still closed. Snapping Styx's leash onto his collar, I let him out. "Where's Retta, Styx?" I asked softly. "Where is she?"

The big old nose went up as he tested the air, and then he was off. I hurried along behind, hoping I didn't slip and break an ankle trying to keep up. He went directly to Critterz, which wasn't surprising, since

Retta had been there more than once. The interesting part was he didn't go up the stairs to the main entrance but dragged me around the building to a hole in the back wall that had recently been covered with boards. At least that's what I surmised from the shiny nail-heads.

"Is he telling us Retta's in there?" Barb asked.

"It seems so." I looked around. "There's a car. Someone's home."

"Take Styx out of sight. I'll go up and knock." I did as she asked, noting that anyone who left the building had to come around front due to the fence at the back.

Climbing the outside staircase, Barb knocked, waited, and knocked again. After some time a woman I hadn't seen before opened the door, Lydia, I guessed, and I heard snatches of their conversation. Lydia was at first cool, then angry. Barb was firm. Lydia's voice rose. "You think your sister is in our building somewhere?"

"I can have the police search if you prefer, but it will be quicker for both of us if you let me see that she isn't inside."

Red spots of anger burned in Lydia's cheeks, but she said, "All right, but you won't find any prisoners here. We're not some fairy tale trio of witches!"

When they went inside I walked around to the front and waited. After a few minutes, a sliding door under the porch opened and Barb gestured me in. I saw a moment of disquiet on Lydia's face when she saw Styx, but she just pressed her lips together more tightly.

The Newf ran into the building with a gusto that told me he expected to find his beloved Retta there. I followed. In a corner that contained the machinery for the freight elevator he paused, straining at the leash. Barb stepped forward to look, bending down for a second, and I sensed Lydia's muscles tensing. "Nothing," Barb finally said, and I pulled Styx away. Though he stopped to sniff several more places, he eventually turned to me as if to say he was sorry to have failed.

"May we look upstairs?" I asked Lydia.

She glared at me with barely-controlled rage. "Do what you want."

I took Styx up the interior staircase, and Barb said, "I'll wait for you here," as we'd agreed. She'd watch the front lot, making sure no one left the old mill unseen. Searching there was difficult, first because the cats reacted to the arrival of a dog in their midst with alarm. There was a great deal of screeching and scrambling, and I held tightly onto the leash in case Styx forgot his purpose and gave chase. He didn't, but the other problem was that the place was literally stuffed with tippable items. We managed not to break anything, and I put the items the dog displaced back as best I could. Lydia followed with arms folded. Finally he turned to me and whined, letting me know he'd found nothing.

"Would you like to look through our personal quarters?" The frost in Lydia's voice said I wouldn't dare.

"Yes, please." I surprised myself, since it was practically accusing her of kidnapping. Rolling her eyes, Lydia led the way upstairs. Styx pushed past her and entered a small sitting room, furnished with a mix of items one or another of the sisters must have chosen from their stock. The only modern things were a large TV mounted on the wall and a computer set up on a beautiful old lawyer's desk.

Betty White sat in an old recliner, working on a Sudoku puzzle. "Well, hello, dear," she said. "We don't have many visitors up here, but it won't take a minute to make some tea."

"She's not staying," Lydia said bluntly. "She's looking for her sister."

Betty's eyes went wide. "Didn't she call you?"

"Yes, but—"

"She isn't here," Lydia interrupted. "Let's get this over with."

Styx made quick work of the apartment, entering the bedrooms, bath, kitchen, and living area without interest. I followed, keeping the leash tight so he didn't upset things. I noticed some boxes on a bed, half-filled with items, and a suitcase in a corner, but nothing that fit my purpose. Retta was not in the building.

Betty's gaze had followed as Styx wandered through the place. When he turned to me, obviously disappointed, she said, "I just know you'll see your sister soon."

Lydia was much less sympathetic. "Are you satisfied?"

I sighed. "Yes. I'm sorry, but—"

"Then get out!" she snapped. "I've been patient because I understand how hard it must be to not know where a family member has gone. But you have to get over this idea that she came here and somehow got locked in like Rapunzel in the tower. If you return, *we* will call the police and swear out a complaint."

"Come on, Styx," I said. Betty gave me a smile and a little hand wave, as if trying to soften her sister's harsh attitude. We bumped down the narrow stairway. "We're sorry to have bothered you."

Lydia merely glared until I took the hint and left.

When we got to the car I put Styx in the back, made sure his feet were on the towels, and climbed in. "Well, that was useless and embarrassing."

"Embarrassing, maybe," Barb said, "but useless, no." From her pocket she took a pair of black stretchy gloves with three pearls at each wrist. "Look familiar?"

"They're Retta's!"

"Styx found them in the corner near the elevator. I hid them so Lydia wouldn't see." Her expression was concerned. "Retta isn't there now, but she was. I'm betting Lars was too."

"Then…" I didn't finish because I was afraid to. If they'd been in the White's storeroom, where were they now? And the deeper, more frightening question: *how* were they?

CHAPTER TWENTY-NINE

Barb

Though I felt like a petitioner pleading for a hearing, I decided we should hunt Agent Stiles down and beg for news. I'd called the number she gave us several times; she'd answered once, informing me in a patronizing tone there was nothing to report and she'd call me when there was. After that my calls went to voicemail. If I showed up at her office with concrete evidence, the gloves I'd found at Critterz, I hoped she'd be less dismissive. In addition, if there were other agency people around, she'd have to at least appear helpful. I looked up the address. The FBI field office was on Broadway, not far from our motel.

Faye suggested I go without her. "Together we look like two old women in search of drama," she said. "Use your big-city lawyer persona, and maybe you'll get better results." She glanced at the dog, adding, "I also think the big guy needs one of us here, or we'll have the neighbors complaining." Styx had grown more anxious since we left the old mill. While we felt the same way, Faye and I didn't resort to howling to express our distress. It took almost constant reassurance to calm him, and being Styx's second-best friend, Faye was the logical person to handle the task.

I hadn't come prepared for the role of VIP, but in Retta's suitcase I found a few things that dressed up my plain black top: a loose sweater-coat in black and green that fell to my hips, (her knees) and a chunky necklace that picked up the gray in my pants and the green in the coat and made an outfit from disparate garments. I'd brought only snow boots and tennis shoes, but in the Midwest in January, everything goes with boots.

The FBI building looked like one would imagine such an edifice should: square, cold, and efficient. The woman at the reception desk, though also square and efficient, was warm. When I told her I was there to see Agent Stiles, she grimaced ruefully. "I'm afraid you're ten minutes too late."

"Do you have any idea what might be a good time for me to return?"

She shook her head. "They had to drive over to Wausau, so it might be late."

"Thanks. Maybe I'll try to catch her in the office tomorrow."

"Him," she corrected with a smile. "He gets that all the time. People think *Jamie* is female, but his parents named him Jamie, not James, so he's stuck with it."

CHAPTER THIRTY

Faye

"If Agent Stiles is a man, who have we been talking to?" I asked when Barb returned from her visit to the FBI office.

"A woman in her thirties." She tapped her chin. "Let's take another look at the grand-daughter Lydia raised."

I couldn't find a recent picture of Kylie Hayworth online, but I brought up the military photo, and we both stared at it for a while.

"With a wig, glasses, and clothes chosen to hide her figure," Barb finally said, "that could be the woman who came here."

"Does that mean nobody's looking for Retta and Lars?"

"No one who believes this is a real emergency." Barb paced, biting her lip. "You said the Whites own a farm. If they needed to move their prisoners someplace remote—"

"I'll find it."

"I'll let Agent Graves know what we've found out. If someone's impersonating an FBI agent, he'll be able to get an investigation going."

But Graves didn't answer his cell. When Barb called the main office in Albuquerque, she learned he was conducting training exercises in the desert. "He's out of cell range, and he probably couldn't hear the phone for all the shooting," the receptionist said. "You can reach him tomorrow, or I can connect you with a different agent if you like."

"I'll call back." Barb hung up, sent Graves a short text, and then said, "I guess we have to try the locals again."

Putting the call on speaker, she called the police department and was connected to the investigations officer she'd spoken to before, Detective Lindeman. I sensed his reserve from the outset as Barb explained what we'd found at Critterz. "Actually, we got a call from Ms. Peete," he said. "She says you forced your way into her place of business and her home with a large dog. She was very uncomfortable, and her older sister was terrified."

"She agreed to let us in to look for Retta," Barb said, but I saw in her expression that we were on shaky legal ground. "And we found my sister's gloves during the search."

Lindeman seemed unconvinced. "She'd been there before. Couldn't she have lost the gloves then?"

Barb made a noncommittal noise, as frustrated as I at the man's refusal to take Retta's disappearance seriously. "Here's the other thing you need to know. A woman has come to our hotel room twice now, claiming to be an FBI agent. We found out this morning she's a fake."

"What does this fake agent want you to do?"

"Nothing. She told us to leave everything to the police."

A pause said Lindeman approved of that advice. "Who do you think this person really is?"

Barb gave me a "here goes" look. "It could be Lydia Peete's granddaughter Kylie."

"Describe her for me."

"Blonde hair, green eyes, plain clothes, pink eyeglasses."

Lindeman made a chuffing laugh. "I know Kylie Hayworth. That doesn't sound like her at all."

"She came in disguise." Barb's voice was strained from the need to remain patient.

"Like you did when you went to Critterz?"

"I did *not* wear a disguise. I just didn't say I was Retta's sister."

"To be honest, ma'am, that's not the way we heard it."

"And you believe your upstanding Green Bay business owners over a couple of out-of-state unknowns."

"I didn't say that, but we do have a bit of she said/she said here." No doubt sensing Barb's frustration, he said, "I talked to the police chief in your home town, and he says you're legitimate investigators. In light of that, I'll ask our sheriff to send a car out to the White family farm. With the snow, it will be easy to tell if someone's been out there."

"We would appreciate that."

"But if we don't find your people there, you should consider that they're headed south, like they said." He tried to lighten his rejection with a chuckle. "This time of year, I don't blame them a bit."

"But Retta hasn't called back or texted. That's very unlike her."

He sighed. "People say they'll call and then don't. It happens a lot when they're on the road."

Knowing we couldn't afford to alienate him, Barb thanked Lindeman, but it was a good thing he couldn't see the look on her face. To me she said "At least he didn't suggest I knit a sweater while I wait for Retta to contact us."

An hour later Lindeman called to report no sign of activity at the old farm. "House is dark. No tracks in the driveway, tires or feet."

"Maybe there's a back way in, or—" Barb stopped, unable to come up with another possibility. We'd been sure the White's old home would provide a lead.

"Ms. Evans, we've got police agencies looking for their vehicles from here to New Mexico. They have descriptions of both Ms. Stilson and Agent Johannsen." After a beat he added, "We've got other things going on around here."

"More important than kidnapped citizens?"

Another beat as he chose his wording. "You've got no proof they were kidnapped, but we for sure had a break-in at Lambeau Field last night. We've got city and county involved, because it looks like the—" He stopped himself from divulging too much information. "It's taking a big share of our manpower to handle it, and the press is all over it." He cleared his throat. "I'll do what I can for you ladies, but I'll bet your sister and her friend will call when they stop for the night."

"You really think Retta hasn't called because she's having too much fun to pick up the phone?"

"Honestly, Ms. Evans. Isn't that more logical than three Green Bay senior citizens capturing not one but two adults who are younger and stronger than all of them put together?"

"But the grandchildren have criminal backgrounds."

He sighed. "Max served his time for whatever he did in New York, and Kye's never been convicted of anything."

"Kye. You know them pretty well?"

Lindeman's tone turned reminiscent. "When I was a sheriff's deputy, I caught young Max blowing up mailboxes. It's supposed to be a federal crime, but when kids lose their parents real sudden like that, they go through some bad times."

"It seems Max is fond of blowing things up."

"He was," Lindeman corrected. "From what I hear, he helps his gram and her sisters a lot these days, fixing things and doing the hauling for the store."

"And where is Kylie?"

"I ran into her at the QuikMart a few months back. Said she was living in Madison and had her own business."

At his indulgent tone, Barb met my gaze and shook her head. I imagined the pretty girl we'd seen in photos smiling up at him while she spun lies. Kylie was a smart cookie. And Grandma Lydia, who'd been smart enough to report our supposedly suspicious behavior to the police in a preemptive strike, was made from the same recipe, just an earlier batch.

CHAPTER THIRTY-ONE

Retta

After my third capture, I was taken—shoved, actually—to the farmhouse. "We'll put you where we can keep an eye on you," Kylie said as we crossed the yard. The walk was painful, since she'd refused to let me get my boots. "One more way to keep you from running." Stocking-footed, I picked my way along frozen tire tracks that twisted and turned all over the place. That walk took cold to a whole new level of frigidity.

"Sit over there." When I took a seat on a straight chair, Max appeared, wearing a parka. "Tie her up," she ordered. "We have to go after Luke."

Max did a fine job with his zip-ties, which I didn't appreciate. Then they left, leaving me uncomfortable and unhappy.

The farmhouse had that overheated ambiance created by a wood stove burning full blast. Kylie and Max had apparently been there for a while, and they'd made a mess of the place. In the kitchen, dishes were piled everywhere and garbage overflowed from a can in the corner. The living room was a cozy space, with afghans over most of the chairs and doilies under each lamp, but Kylie's suitcase lay open on the couch, clothing spilling over the edge, and a pair of battered tennis shoes sat near the stove, drying as they added the stench of feet to the room.

As I waited, helpless, for their return, I thought of Luke, who'd thrown me to the wolves but probably didn't know the area well enough to escape two locals. I also thought of Lars. The root cellar would be below the frost-line, where the temperature was milder than outside, but it still wouldn't be pleasant down there.

When Kylie returned several hours later, her cheeks were red with cold, but her expression revealed satisfaction. That and the fact that Luke didn't join us made me suspect things hadn't gone well for him. Taking a seat on an old armchair between me and the doorway, she laid her hand atop the padded arm so the gun was a visible threat. "You don't give up easy, do you?"

"It's not like there's a chance you won't kill me if I stick around."

Her brow arched. "Well, at least you're not stupid."

"According to Luke, you already killed someone."

"I didn't mean to." Her mouth twisted like a child caught fibbing. "I didn't ask your boyfriend to stick his nose into my business either."

"Your *business* is illegal. Any law officer would try to stop you."

"Well, he isn't going to. This is something we've worked our whole lives for."

I couldn't contain my curiosity or curb my tongue. "What's worth involving your whole family in capital crimes?"

At first I didn't think she'd tell me, but it felt like she wanted to share. "You figured out that we deal in special goods."

"Stolen," I corrected.

"Whatev." She rolled her eyes. "A month ago I got a line on some goods that sounded interesting. An old guy from Illinois, some sort of military contractor in Iraq back in the day, had sent a bunch of stuff home under the radar."

"Items stolen from their national museum."

A quirk of her brows allowed that might be true. "It was little stuff: jewelry with a few semi-precious stones, small statues, like that." She twisted in the chair, pulling her feet up. "So the guy died. I offered the son a price for the whole shebang, and he accepted it." Her lips closed tightly for a moment before she went on. "While we were carrying the stuff to my van, this wooden puzzle box slid off the pile, hit the tile floor, and broke open. Inside was a necklace like nothing I saw before."

"Gold?"

"Yeah, but more than that." Rising, she left the room and returned with a box. She opened it, took out a velvet bag, and slid the necklace out into her hand. An intricate mesh of delicate gold flowers with stones at the center of each, the piece was stunningly beautiful. "Those are rubies, sapphires, and emeralds," Kylie said, pointing as she spoke. "It's from the reign of Suleiman the Magnificent, who I never heard of before, but he was a pretty important guy."

"He controlled large portions of Europe and Asia in the 1500s." Again, romance novels can be instructive.

A roll of her shoulders said details didn't matter. "So the necklace is worth a gazillion, and I had it." Her face darkened. "I should have."

"The heir objected to including the necklace with the other items."

"He did." She pushed her hair back from her face in an impatient gesture. "What was I supposed to do, give it back? *He* called *me*." Her face darkened with anger. "He *said* he wanted it *gone*. I *paid* him!"

"That might be valid, *if* the goods in question were his to sell."

A head shake dismissed that. "He got all up in my face. Said the necklace was his. Said all I bought was the box so I could glue it back together and sell it." Her face tightened.

"You killed him."

As if to punish me, she slid the necklace back into the bag and closed it inside the box. "He tried to grab the necklace. I had the box in my other hand, and I hit him with it, not even very hard." Her chin wobbled briefly, but she shoved her conscience back to where she wanted it. "He *started* it."

"And Luke?"

She rolled her eyes. "Loser Luke should have stayed in Madison."

With that she left the room, allowing me to draw my own conclusions. Kylie was an in-for-a-penny,-in-for-a-pound type girl, and like her grandmother, anything she had to do was justified by twisted logic. If more murders could help them escape capture, I had no doubt either of them would do whatever was required.

CHAPTER THIRTY-TWO

Faye

At noon on Wednesday, Barb and I walked to the little diner we'd been frequenting for meals. Neither of us felt much like eating, but it often helps in times of crisis to behave normally. At the least, regular meals keep people ready for action—if they can decide what action to take.

"What if I talk to Betty one-on-one?" I asked, pouring ranch dressing on my potatoes. "We agree she's probably unaware of how bad things are, but I'm sure she knows things she doesn't know she knows, just from being there every day."

"They won't let her talk to us now that we've made it clear we suspect them."

"True." I ate my hot beef sandwich, but not with my usual enjoyment while Barb toyed with a salad. "I just don't know what to try next." Retta had been missing for three days, Lars for four. It was hard to stay positive, and prayer didn't feel like enough at this point.

When we neared the motel I heard Styx, his voice raised in a howl I'd never heard him make until this week. *I know how you feel, boy. Lost and useless.* "I'm sure Mr. Hauer has been hearing about Styx from the other guests. I'll take him for a walk."

Barb shook her head. "It's about all you can do right now."

We weren't twenty steps from the motel when my phone rang. The caller ID said it was Celia, and I braced for yet another assault from the Burner sisters.

"Hi, Faye, are you busy?"

"As a matter of fact, I am."

"Well, I won't keep you long then. I just wondered if you knew what Wanda and the others are up to."

"I can't imagine." My sarcasm was lost on Celia, but then, any sort of subtlety was useless with her. Celia was the family member who played one side against the other, offering secrets in order to get someone to say mean things she could then carry back to her sisters.

"Well, they got a lawyer, and they're gonna try to break Ma's will. Can you believe that?"

I chose a response that gave her no ammunition. "Huh."

"Wanda says Dale made her give her place to the church because he's mad at us, and you'll be big shots with the pastor and everybody."

"Huh."

"I think that's mean of her to say that. Don't you think it's mean?"

A note of frustration in Celia's voice told me I was doing well thus far, but a direct question required a response. "I think it's always sad when family members disagree."

"Yeah," she thought she had something going. "It isn't right for Wanda and them to attack Dale like that. He's our brother, and I think he should do what he wants. He's had it really rough." She paused before delivering her best shot. "I bet you'd like to punch Wanda in the nose, right?"

"Of course not. You're Dale's sisters, and he loves you. I'm sure things will work out in the end."

"Oh."

"Now as I said, I've got a lot going on, so I'll let you go. Thanks for calling."

Stuffing the phone in my pocket, I said to Styx, "Let's go, buddy. I need a stress-relieving walk as much as you do."

We took the route that had become our habit: across the motel lot, down a street, and into the park along the river. Styx seemed slightly less anxious outside, and I thought how nice it would be to be a dog and have no fears for the future. The Newf didn't have to deal with petty relatives. He didn't know Retta might be dead or dying. I did. As we walked, tears began to leak out my eyes. At first I wiped them away, but they came stronger and faster, and soon I was unable to keep from sobbing aloud. Seeing no one nearby, I pulled Styx to a stop, wiped the snow off a bench, and sat down to let my sorrow out. The dog stuck his nose under my arm and licked my face, whining in accompaniment.

We must have sat like that longer than I realized, because a voice made me jump in surprise. "Are you okay, ma'am?"

Turning, I saw a good-looking man of about thirty-five standing a few feet away. Dressed in jeans, a baggy sweatshirt, and a leather jacket, he had two dogs with him, a small spaniel and a friendly-looking mutt. Both strained at their leashes, eager to investigate Styx. As he held them back, the man's eyes rested on me with concern.

"I'm all right," I told him, wiping away my tears. "Some...bad things are happening, and...They got to me for a second."

The stranger nodded. "Sometimes life is like that."

Though the guy had a nice smile, I'm not one to drop my troubles onto someone else's shoulders. "Nice dogs," I commented.

"That's Chance, and this is Frankie," he said, pointing. "They've been cooped up in my truck while I took care of some stuff, so I thought I'd let them have a run before we head home."

"I know what you mean." I patted Styx. "This big guy is staying with me in a very small motel room."

He chuckled. "Now that sounds like trouble! How'd you get the biggest dog available?"

"He belongs to my sister."

"Then you're dog-sitting?"

I shared a little bit of my agony. "My sister is missing, but I don't think the police here believe that. Plus they're busy with some crime at Lambeau Field, which I guess is a big deal around here."

"Yes," he said. "That's actually why I'm in town today."

I looked up from untangling the leash Styx had wrapped around a lamppost. "You're with the Packers?"

There was that smile again. "Yes. I'm sorry if our break-in has diverted attention from your sister's disappearance."

"Well, there isn't much either of us can do about it."

"I wish I could help."

He seemed genuinely concerned, and an idea came into my head that was so Retta-like, so outrageous and dramatic, that I almost heard her whispering in my ear: *You want Betty to talk to you. Betty loves anything to do with the Green Bay Packers.* "Could you spare an hour to help me find her?"

He glanced toward Lambeau Field. "I guess so. Things are on hold until the police finish their crime-scene stuff."

"And you really work for the Packers?"

"I do."

"Are you someone a fan would recognize?" When he hesitated I admitted, "I'm not a follower of professional sports."

His answer came with a funny little smile. "I think most people around here know who I am."

I almost didn't say my idea aloud, but then I asked myself, *What can it hurt to try?*

"Here's the thing. I know of a person who might help me find my sister. This...witness...is a huge Packer fan, so if someone from the team asked her to tell what she knows, she might do it."

He frowned. "She's a kidnapper?"

"No. She *knows* the kidnappers, but she's...naive, I guess is the word for it."

The man's frown deepened, and I realized what a strange thing I'd asked of him. Feeling my face flush I said, "Never mind. I shouldn't have brought it up."

He glanced toward Lambeau. "How far would we need to go?"

"It's actually pretty close, now that I'm getting to know my way around." Hoping to relieve any fears he might have about my intentions I added, "We could drive our own vehicles."

He thought about it. "I'll give it a shot."

"Thanks so much." Rising from the bench, I took a firm hold on Styx's leash and pulled him away from Chance and Frankie. "I'll get the car, meet you back here, and you can follow me to Barry Street. I promise I won't keep you long." I stopped, thinking again how weird this was. "I guess I should introduce myself. I'm Faye Burner, and you're—?"

Again that funny smile. "My girlfriend calls me Green Bay."

When we reached the old mill, I drove around to the back and saw Betty putting some things into a PT Cruiser. I was beyond pleased to catch her alone, but luck just had to go my way once in a while.

When the man got out of his truck, her eyes got big. Guessing she thought I'd brought along some muscle I said, "I'm not here to make trouble. My friend wanted to meet you after I told him you're a big—"

Betty wasn't listening. "Oh my god," she said. "You're—"

"—Really happy to meet you," Green Bay said. "Faye here tells me you're a big Packer fan."

Her face practically glowed. "The biggest," she replied. "I can name every coach from Curly to now, and every quarterback, every field goal kicker, and most of the D-line if they're any good."

"That's great." There followed a conversation I won't even begin to try to repeat, because it meant nothing to me. Terms like *five-step drop* and *free agent strategy* were tossed in, and I tuned out for a while, trying to hide my impatience. Green Bay knew what he was doing though, because Betty ate it up. When he finally turned the subject to my situation, she was emotionally unable to resist his questions.

"Now Faye here is missing her sister, and I bet someone as smart as you knows where she might be. Am I right?"

"I—I," She wanted to lie but couldn't bring herself to do it. "She's going to be fine. Soon everything will be straightened out." She turned to me. "Your sister will come back to you. She's just been really busy for a while."

"Busy?"

"Yes." She liked the sound of that and said again, "Busy. We had things to do, but tomorrow they'll be done, and she'll come walking right through your door."

Though I didn't believe a word of it, I sensed Betty thought she was telling the truth.

"How do you know Retta's okay?" I asked, but Betty just repeated that I'd see her tomorrow. When I pressed again for Retta's location, she seemed about to panic. Sensing her fear, Green Bay stepped in to talk football again. After a few minutes on recent rule changes and referee criticism Betty said, "Oh, I wish I had my phone. I'd love a photo with you."

Green Bay got his out and had me take a picture of him with Betty, his arm around her shoulders and her face pink with joy. "Where shall I send it?" he asked, and she put her contact information into his phone, her fingers clumsy with what I could only think of as awe. Grateful to Green Bay, I was also struck by the oddness of getting information from an accessory to kidnapping by appealing to her love of a football team.

"Betty! You're needed inside." Lydia had come out onto the porch, and she glared down at us. With her head sunk to her chest Betty went up the steps and slid by Lydia as if afraid she might get slapped. Under Lydia's angry glare I thanked my new friend for his help. Assuring me it had been "interesting," he and his dogs left in his sporty pickup. Lydia remained in place, a stony statue, until I got into the car, turned it around, and drove away.

CHAPTER THIRTY-THREE

Barb

While Faye was out on some mysterious mission that involved taking my car and leaving Styx with me, I got a call from Agent Graves in Albuquerque.

"I've found something you aren't going to like."

"Tell me."

"The police in Illinois interviewed Kylie Hayworth two weeks ago. A man she'd had business with was found dead, and his wife said Ms. Hayworth was there when she left home to do some errands."

"How did he die?"

"Someone cracked him in the head with an unspecified wooden object. Ms. Hayworth told the police she'd gone there to pick up stuff from an estate. Nothing unusual happened. He helped her load the stuff into her van, she paid him for it and left. Neighbors saw him helping her carry things out, but no one saw him alive after she left."

"Do you think she killed the man?"

"Nobody can think of a reason why she would. They made a deal. She got the stuff. He got cash."

"The money was there?"

"Yes. Seven hundred dollars and change. The wife thought that was the amount her husband mentioned he'd be getting."

"And did someone look at the stuff she bought from him?"

"Souvenirs from the Middle East. That interested me, given what we suspect Lars saw."

"But nothing in this guy's stuff was valuable enough to kill for."

"Not that we know of. The detective did mention that when he got to her hotel room, Ms. Hayworth was in the shower. She came to the door in a towel, which he found distracting. I wondered why she was taking a shower at eleven a.m."

"Huh."

"I know, it's thin," he said, "but what if Kylie killed the guy to get her hands on some item we don't know about? She lied her way out of it, but if Lars had reported the stolen goods he saw, the whole bunch of them would have come under scrutiny."

"But if they killed or kidnapped Lars, they must know it's all going to fall apart soon. When he and Retta don't arrive in Albuquerque, the police will come back to the place he was last seen."

"They've got to run, but it looks like they also want to sell whatever Kylie got from the man in Illinois."

"And hide their tracks before they disappear completely from Green Bay." I sighed. "What do we do now?"

"I've started a hunt for Kylie in Madison. I also tried to contact the real Jamie Stiles to give him a heads-up, but we played phone tag all day. I'll try again tomorrow before I head out to the training grounds." Graves paused, adding, "We still can't prove any of this, but every hour we don't hear from Lars or Retta makes a more convincing case."

And every hour means it's less likely they're alive, I thought. Aloud I said, "Thanks for your help, Bill. I'll be in touch."

When Faye returned, she told me about asking one of the Green Bay Packers to go with her to talk to Betty. "She was so impressed that she as much as admitted she knows where Retta is."

"You found a Green Bay Packer and took him to the old mall?"

"Yes. We met in the park and we both had dogs, and—" She shrugged, as if the result was the most natural thing in the world.

"Who was this guy?"

She made a helpless gesture. "You know I don't pay attention to athletes. Betty was impressed, and he looked like someone I've seen on TV. Something about a pickup that gets hit by a drone?"

That made me blink, but I didn't push it. Faye's action had been a little brilliant, a little reckless. It was something Retta would have done in a heartbeat, and it seemed like her spirit had taken over, infusing Faye with boldness. Though I was surprised by what she'd done, it buoyed my mood to hear that Betty had indicated Retta was still alive.

I reported my conversation with Graves, and Faye pressed her fingers to her lips for a second. "Betty was putting stuff into the back of their car when we got there. And yesterday when Styx and I went upstairs to search, the apartment looked half-empty."

"They're getting out."

She nodded. "That's what Betty meant about tomorrow being the end of their busy time. She thinks Retta and Lars will be released when they leave town."

"I don't."

"No." Faye stirred, anxious to take action. "Barb, we have to find them before tomorrow morning. After that, we'll be too late."

CHAPTER THIRTY-FOUR

Retta

Over the course of Wednesday, I learned bits and pieces of what Kylie had planned for the next morning. The kitchen wasn't far from where I was tied, and Kye and Max spent most of their time there. One of them was a big eater, so pans rattled, cupboard doors opened and closed, and food smells emanated that made my stomach growl. If they heard, it didn't engender any sympathy for my plight. Neither of them was a nurturer, like their Aunt Betty was.

First they congratulated themselves for having caught Luke. "You were something," Kylie told Max. "Just like a bird dog, flushing him out and turning him so he came right toward me."

"I figured he'd go for the road eventually," Max said proudly, "so I just waited until he showed and then cut him off."

"You did really good." Her tone was overly expressive, and I concluded that, like the older generation, she fed Max scraps of praise as rewards for his crimes. Not that he had any qualms about breaking the law, but he seemed to operate on approval from his family.

"I still think we should blow up the mill." Max's tone was half regretful, half hopeful. "I had it all worked out."

"Do you think you could do that here instead?"

A few seconds of thought. "Yeah, I could, I guess."

"We'd need it to look like an accident."

"Why? This ain't our place, so who cares if it blows up?"

Kylie's tone was patient. "Because they're going to find a dead FBI agent in the rubble."

"Oh. Yeah."

"If it doesn't look planned, they can wonder what he was doing out here, but they won't know for sure."

"What about the bullet hole in Luke?"

"Who's to say the fed didn't kill him? We'll mess up the wound and fire the agent's gun then leave it beside him."

"You sure are good at figuring things out," Max said admiringly.

"I have to be." Kylie's voice revealed pride in her own cleverness. "But those people just keep coming. The two nosy old bats are still hanging around somewhere."

"I sent 'em to Manitowoc, but I guess that didn't work."

"It was a good idea though. Gram did her part, calling the local Leos and saying those women waved a gun in her face and scared her."

"And you thought of playing FBI agent. Where'd you get the badge and stuff?"

"With Cosplay as big as it is right now, you can get anything like that, even in Green Bay." It sounded like she smirked a little. "We haven't got rid of them, but we did slow them down."

"It'll all be okay tomorrow."

"Yeah. Gram told everyone they're moving to some retirement community. In the morning I'll meet my guy and trade the necklace for cash. Can you get this place ready to blow?"

A chair scraped. "Let me go look at something."

Steps sounded on a staircase. I heard Kylie sip at a drink, possibly coffee with vanilla creamer. Then Max returned. "We got some good luck. There's a gravity unit down there."

"What's that?"

"An old gas furnace with a bad reputation. The pilots can fail if they get wet or get blown out or whatever."

"Which could make them explode?"

"Big-time." Max sounded excited about the prospect.

"And you can make the pilot fail?"

Now he sounded almost offended. "Well, sure."

"Maxie, you are the best problem solver ever. Tomorrow morning we'll put Luke in a closet somewhere, like they had him locked up. Then we'll set the fed and his girlfriend in the living room with that old witch Charmaine."

"I could bring Luke in now."

"Think about that, Max. Isn't he better off out in the cold?"

"Right, right. Don't want him smelling up the place."

"Before we leave, we'll set up a little tableau."

"Tab what?"

"Tableau. It's a scene that looks real but isn't."

"I get it," Max said excitedly. "The FBI guy and his girlfriend on the couch, the old lady in the rocker. Like they were talking about stuff and then the place just went up."

"Right." After a beat Kylie said, "I hope Gram doesn't let Aunt Dee putz around too long. And I told her not to let Betty bring a bunch of extra crap."

"You know she's going to want all her football stuff."

"Gram's gonna tell her it's already packed. She hopes Betty will forget about it in a week or two."

Max snuffled derisively. "Like she's forgot everything else in the last few months."

CHAPTER THIRTY-FIVE

Barb

"I've looked everywhere I can think of," Faye said dejectedly. "There's no other property in the state associated with the Whites." After a second she added, "It's going to get really cold tonight."

I checked my watch. Almost five-thirty. "I could try calling Agent Graves again. He might be back from the training grounds."

Faye shook her head. "Let's drive out to that farm ourselves and see what we can find."

"It's getting dark. And the police say there's no one out there."

"But we've got Styx. When it comes to locating someone he loves, a dog's sense of smell is amazing."

Though I wasn't as certain as Faye of Styx's abilities, it was better than staring at each other across our tiny space. "I'll let Rory know, so someone is aware of where we are."

"I know I don't have to tell you to be careful," Rory said when I called. "These people are dangerous."

"All the more reason we need to find Lars and Retta."

He couldn't argue with that. "Okay. If I don't hear from you in two hours, I'm calling in the cavalry."

"That sounds fair."

Faye had once again blanketed my cargo area to prevent it being coated with dog hair. Styx climbed happily into the back. I brought along Retta's tablet, which I connected to my on-board wi-fi.

Following GPS directions, we left the city and turned off a state road onto a tertiary one called Balsam. About a mile down was the White place, but we saw immediately the police had reported correctly. No one had been in or out of the driveway in some time. The house, a one-story structure, was snow-covered and blank-looking. Two small outbuildings slanted to the side, in danger of imminent collapse. Nothing moved. Nothing looked like it had *been* moved in some time.

I pulled the car to the side of the road. "Well, that's a bust."

"I was so hopeful." Faye sounded close to tears. "I'm going to roll down the window a little and let Styx have a sniff." As she did it she said, "Styx, where's Retta? Where is she?"

The big guy stuck his head out, testing the air from right to left. It took a few seconds, but he got excited, pushing at the window until I feared he'd break through it. "Down, Styx. Sit!" Faye grabbed his collar to hold him back. Having a dog with glass shards in his chest would only add to our troubles.

"Retta is close," Faye said, though her voice wavered from her efforts to keep him still. "He wouldn't go off like that for no reason."

I had to bite my tongue. *Styx?* I wanted to say. *Styx goes off for a dozen reasons, from squirrels to UPS trucks to random moonbeam emanations.* Faye needed to believe he was leading us in the right direction.

Honestly, so did I.

183

Firing up the iPad, I brought up a satellite image of the area. "There's a house in the trees about a half mile back, on the other side of the road."

"The Whites would know where the empty houses are."

"Actually, I doubt they'd choose an empty one," I said. "They'd want a place that's occupied, so people wouldn't get suspicious about lights in the windows or tracks in the drive."

"Let me have that tablet." After a few seconds Faye said, "Here. The house at 15 Balsam Road belongs to Charmaine Dahlman, who's seventy-two."

I made a U-turn and went back, turning off my headlights before we got there. In the drive of the old farmhouse were three vehicles, a prim-looking sedan, a dark van, and a flatbed truck. "That truck was at the old mill," Faye said.

"Is Mrs. Dahlman in on this, or have they taken over her house?"

"I would guess she's a prisoner. How many larcenous senior citizens can there be in the greater Green Bay area?"

"I wouldn't even speculate," I replied. "But if she isn't one of them, that makes three people in need of rescue."

CHAPTER THIRTY-SIX

Retta

I knew I couldn't just eavesdrop on Kylie and Max all day, though I didn't have a lot of other options. My ankles were fastened to the chair's front legs and my wrists to the back uprights, just above the seat. Sitting in one position for hours had made my whole body ache, but moving my hands or feet caused the ties to cut into my skin. Other than shifting my weight and rotating my shoulders, I could do nothing to alleviate my discomfort. I needed to get out of the chair. In no position to do those maneuvers they show on Facebook that break zip-ties like magic, I could only do one thing: wriggle.

The chair was old, and over time the glue that holds furniture together becomes brittle. Rocking the chair back and forth should pull its separate pieces apart, though I couldn't say how long that would take. It was the only move I had, but Max was depressingly vigilant, checking on me often and making cracks about how I wasn't so quick at escaping this time.

Kylie too came by a few times and stopped to look me over, but she seemed to assume I wasn't going anywhere. Whenever I was alone, I wrenched the chair back and forth as violently as possible. When one of them came by I sat still, apparently dejected, with my head hung low. Alone again, I returned to my sitting-dance, establishing a rhythm. Jerk until footsteps approach. Stop and look defeated. Jerk again. Stop. Repeat.

After dinner (I got nothing, but they had some kind of pasta), I heard Kylie talking on the phone. When she hung up she told Max in a weary tone, "Gram says they have more than they can fit in the car. Take the truck into town and get their stuff."

"I could just take the van, so we don't have to move it twice."

"In the first place, I intend to sort through and dump about two-thirds of what they think is essential," Kylie replied. "In the second place, that van isn't tied to any of us, so I don't want it seen anywhere near the old mill."

"Okay." The door slammed and Max roared off. That was a good thing, because I was almost completely free to work on destroying the chair while Kylie played some tweet-y game on her phone.

Sometime later, when the sun had gone down and the windows turned black, the chair frame started making ominous squeaks. Craning my neck, I saw that the joints on the seat had opened up more than half an inch. The rungs connecting the legs were loose as well, and I tried to imagine what was going to happen. The chair might break apart completely and I'd crash to the floor. One set of legs might come loose, which would tip me onto my side. In either case I had to get free of bits of chair as quickly as possible and find either an escape route or a hiding place. I saw no spot in the room to hide, and escape didn't look promising either, since Kylie was between me and the exit. The room's three double-hung windows had frames thickly covered with a chalky, hideous blue paint, which hinted they'd be difficult, maybe impossible, to open. If it was my only way out, I'd jump through.

As I considered that, I caught a flash of movement at one corner of the pitted glass. Squinting to penetrate the darkness, I saw a face, and pale hair caught the interior light. Lars!

He mouthed something, but I couldn't see well enough to read his lips. I answered with a silent, "Wait!" and demonstrated that I was

186

working on getting free. He nodded with an exaggerated head movement and brandished something that looked like a magic wand. After a moment I realized it was a crowbar.

A rumble outside indicated Max was back with the truck. Hearing Kylie's footsteps I mouthed, "Wait!" again just before she appeared in the doorway, stopped to give me a long look, and then moved on to the kitchen. I heard Max come inside. "They're not far behind me," he told her. "I've got their stuff on the truck. I was right about Aunt Betty and the Packer stuff. There's boxes and boxes of it."

"Okay." It sounded like Kylie was putting on boots. "We'll move the minimum to the van before they get here. The rest you can dump in a trash bin on your way back to town."

Max had a wistful proposal. "I could still go back and rig the mill to blow. I guarantee they won't find any evidence."

Kylie sighed. "Two explosions in one night, Max? You don't think that would look suspicious?"

Max sighed too. "I guess."

The kitchen door opened, and a draft of cold air hit my knees. "I'll sort," Kylie said as they left. "You can hide—"

The rest was lost as the door closed. "Lars! Now!"

Lars applied the pry-bar to the windowsill and wrenched until the sash slid up a couple of inches. Once he'd opened a gap, he pushed the window up as far as it would go, about two-thirds.

The chair was close to separating, but I couldn't wait. As soon as the opening was big enough I hopped, chair and all, toward it, tilted forward like a runner at the starting line. Lars reached in, grasped the chair seat, and lifted me through. He set me on the ground then turned to close the window to mask my escape route. I rattled the chair some more, and the seat separated from the back. That made things worse, since my hands were attached to one part and my feet to another.

A figure emerged from the dark, ordering, "Be still for a minute."

Surprised, I obeyed, and a woman of perhaps seventy cut the zip ties with pruning shears, tossing chair pieces aside as she went. "There. Can you run?"

I was already feeling the cold on the soles of my feet, chilling my blood, but I nodded.

"This way." She started off into the dark side of the yard.

As we followed Lars whispered, "She owns this place, and she'll find us a hiding spot."

I wasn't convinced of that. Our captors could follow our footprints in the snow, as they'd probably done to track Luke down. Still, I was free and I was with Lars. Under those circumstances, I was willing to aim for an optimistic view.

CHAPTER THIRTY-SEVEN

Faye

"Let's do a little scouting," I told Barb. "We need to know the situation."

"We should call the police." She peered anxiously into the dark.

"Agreed, but it would help if we could tell them who's there and where they are." Though she knew I was right, I saw resistance in her eyes. "In the time it takes for the police to get here, I can slide through those trees and get a good look at the house." When she still hesitated I said, "I'll take Styx for protection, and I won't engage, just report."

"Okay, but I expect you back here in ten minutes." She pulled a pistol from her coat pocket. "It's Lars' service weapon," she said. "If you're not back, I'll come for you."

"We'll be back," I said. "Styx will find Retta."

She glanced at the dog, who danced with impatience. "What if he barks?"

I grinned. "Girl, you've been a city-dweller for too long." Barb frowned, and I assured her, "In the country dogs bark all the time. Nobody pays much attention."

Taking a flashlight from her glovebox, she handed it to me. "Keep it off unless you absolutely have to use it," she ordered. "No sense making yourself a target."

Considering the wooded area we'd be traversing, a leash for Styx would be more hindrance than help. Taking a firm grip on his collar, I started toward the trees.

I was knee-deep in snow when my phone buzzed. Stopping, I took it from my pocket and read the caller ID. *Wanda.* I pressed the button that said I wasn't taking calls at present and put the phone in silent mode. Though she certainly hadn't meant to, Wanda had done me a favor. Closer to the house, the buzz of my phone might have betrayed my presence and gotten me into trouble.

Styx pulled me along, which I took for certainty that Retta was somewhere ahead. While I'd promised Barb we'd stay away from the bad guys, I wasn't sure Styx understood that a straight-on assault wasn't a good idea. If Retta was on the property, he'd be willing to run over anyone who stood in his way to get to her. My job was to make sure he was a locator, not a rescuer—at least, not yet.

CHAPTER THIRTY-EIGHT

Barb

I called the Fox County police and reported a possible hostage situation. The revelation was met with professional doubt. "Can you explain why you believe that, ma'am?"

"There are a lot of tracks going in and out of the driveway," I told the man on duty, "but the owner's car hasn't moved in days, judging by the snow covering."

"What makes you think there are hostages?"

"There are four cars in the driveway."

"That could mean a party. Did you see someone with a weapon?"

"No. We can't see anyone at all."

"Did you hear something? A commotion or people screaming?"

I sighed. "No."

His voice took on a different tone. "Who am I speaking with?"

"Barbara Evans. We've been looking for our sister, and we're almost certain she's being held prisoner out here, along with a federal agent and the owner of the house."

"And the people responsible are three old women who own an antique shop in town, right?"

I bit my lip before answering so I wouldn't snap at him. "They have relatives with criminal pasts. We believe—"

My argument sounded ridiculous, even to me. *We believe a trio of old women has been involved in small-time crime in your area for years but has now graduated to kidnapping and murder for reasons we don't understand.* How had the Whites become criminals? Which of them were guilty and which innocent? Why had they kidnapped Lars? How could I convince this man they were holed up in a neighbor's home, waiting for a nebulous event we suspected but couldn't prove? I couldn't answer a single one of those questions, but I sensed Retta was here.

Rather than argue, I took a formal tone, "I'm requesting a wellness check on Charmaine Dahlman at 33 Balsam Road."

"Hold, please." The man conferred with someone else then said, "We're sending a car, ma'am. Please don't take any action. The deputy will handle it."

Ending that call, I made a second one, this time to the Green Bay FBI office. "I believe Agent Johannsen and at least two others are being held at this address," I told the person who answered. "Agent Graves of the Albuquerque office is aware of the situation, and I believe he spoke with Agent Stiles."

"I'll relay the information to him," she said, then gave me the same line I'd heard from the sheriff's officer. "Don't attempt anything until help arrives."

"Got it." Putting my phone away, I peered into the darkness, trying to figure a timeline. The sheriff's office would send a deputy. I would make him listen to our arguments and send for reinforcements. Stiles would probably take longer to respond, but he would add his influence, even if he couldn't come himself, and urge the sheriff to act.

Turning the phone back on, I checked the time. Seven minutes had passed since Faye left with Styx. I thought about calling the Green Bay police. Rory had talked to their chief and vouched for us, but I wasn't sure that had been passed on to the county officers. Jokes about hysterical women with conspiracy theories would travel quickly through the ranks. Confirmation of our competence from an objective source wasn't nearly so entertaining. It would take longer to filter through.

What would I do if Faye didn't return in three minutes? Make noise? Drive up to the house and pretend to be lost? Three minutes later, I checked my phone again. Except it wasn't three minutes. It was only forty seconds. Waiting is the hardest thing there is.

That's when the shooting started, and all bets were off.

We'd parked on the road, some distance back from the farmhouse. My choices were to follow Faye's path through the trees or enter via the driveway, where I could be seen—and possibly shot—from a long way off. I chose the route with cover.

Despite the fact that Faye had broken trail, it felt like a mile to the edge of the woods. I soon lost any possible stealth advantage due to heavy breathing and constant sniffling. When the tracks turned sharply right, away from the house, I guessed Styx had found Retta's trail. That gave me renewed vigor, and I struggled on.

There were no more shots, which was a relief. At the edge of the trees I stopped, surveying the farm from a much closer vantage point. I was on a rise, with an old barn to my right and the rest of the farm below. Moonlight showed tracks running everywhere, and the vehicle responsible for them, a 4-wheeler, parked next to what looked like cellar doors alongside the farmhouse. Interior lights burned, showing the place was occupied. A halogen yard light revealed nothing moving outside.

A single bark—more like a yelp—sounded from inside the barn, and I turned to look. The loft door stood open, only a few yards away. If Styx had led Faye there, it might mean Retta was in the barn. Cautiously, I moved forward.

Approaching the open door, I stopped and peered into the darkness. I felt a jerk at my hand, and the gun I held was twisted from my grip. A voice much too cheerful for the situation said, "You ain't the one I was after, but I guess you'll do."

CHAPTER THIRTY-NINE

Faye

The first shot surprised me, and for a second I didn't know what I'd heard. A second followed, and Styx strained against my grip, ready to dash to the rescue. I held him back, though I wasn't sure what was best. Letting Styx loose might help Retta, but he might be wounded or even killed.

But if we didn't interrupt whatever disaster was happening, Retta or Lars might be murdered.

Styx was one hundred percent sure what he wanted to do. Even if I could have told him he might die if he rushed to Retta's side, he'd have taken the chance anyway.

Crouching, I took Styx' big head in my two hands. "Find Retta," I whispered as he wriggled to get free and do just that. "But be careful, okay, big guy?"

That part didn't register, and when I let go of his head, he ran as if pursued by demons.

The area around the barn had been plowed. I followed Styx, staying in the shadows. Peering ahead, I saw his rear end disappear into the hayloft, where a door stood open. I stole up, set my back to the wall, and listened. Styx gave an impatient bark that seemed to ask what I was waiting for. Most of the inside was dark, but in a spill of moonlight from an open window I saw two objects tossed carelessly on the floor. Retta's boots. She was here, but she was barefoot.

I followed Styx inside, stopping to pick up the boots. Styx ran ahead, and suddenly I heard the scratch of nails and then a thud, a grunt, and a yelp. "Styx!"

For a second there was nothing. Then I heard him whimper, but the sound came from below me. Carefully I moved through the darkness, testing the ground ahead with my feet. When my foot touched only air, I knew what had happened. Styx had fallen through a trapdoor used for dropping hay to the livestock below.

Getting down on my knees, I fished the flashlight out of my pocket and turned it on. The slender beam revealed an overturned gas can, a pitchfork, and a single cow looking up at me with a curious tilt to her head. "Styx?" My answer was a second whine. I couldn't see him, but he was down there, alive. That was all I could tell.

Should I lower myself through the hole? That wasn't a great idea. If there was no exit on that level, I'd never be able to pull myself back up through the hole. I had to approach the problem from outside. I stood, ready to do that, but sounds at the doorway caused me to freeze. I heard a woman's grunt of pain and objection, followed by a man's voice. A second later he called into the barn, "I got your sister, lady. You'd better come out of there."

CHAPTER FORTY

Retta

Charmaine moved confidently across her yard, her speed and agility a testament to farming as a healthy lifestyle. Lars and I followed in a crouch, going from one bit of cover to the next and staying out of the light as much as possible. I felt like there was a target on my back, and my worst fears were realized when a shot rang out. Turning, I tried to see where it came from, but Lars urged, "Keep going!" When a second shot sounded, I realized they weren't aimed in our direction. Someone was firing blindly into the dark in hopes we'd give ourselves away by taking off in panic. That was a good possibility where I was concerned. My happy place was as far away from that gun as possible.

We caught up with Charmaine when she stopped at an odd-looking building I recognized as a corn crib, a ten-by-eight shed with a tight roof, sturdy door, and gaps between the boards that let air circulate to dry the cobs of corn over time. "In here," she ordered, releasing a hook from an eye and holding the door open. Lars went first and started burrowing out a space at the back of the crib. I looked around, doubtful this was our best choice for a hiding place. "They'll follow our tracks in the snow."

"They go every which way." Looking back, I saw that tracks did indeed circle the crib, barn, and house, with trails bending into the trees at several spots. "I feed my cows every day, and the deer too, so they even go off into the woods." Climbing the two steps, I crouched through the low doorway and joined Lars at the back, helping him open up a space for the three of us to sit on the wooden floor. Charmaine stopped to reach a hand through the slats by the door. Fumbling briefly, she maneuvered the hook back into the eye. Then she joined us. Noticing she wore no coat, I moved over and let her sit between Lars and me.

After what seemed like a long time we'd heard footsteps approaching. Through the slats I saw a bright light. The steps slowed at the corn crib, and the light washed over the door, but after only a few seconds went on. From the muttering I concluded our pursuer was Max. We sat for some time in silence, hardly daring to breathe.

When she was sure he was gone Charmaine whispered, "The trail winds all over in the trees. He'll soon give up and go back to the house."

Lars put an eye up to the slats. "All I can see is the side of the house where the door is." A beat later he said, "Oh-oh."

"What?" I inserted myself under his chin in order to get the same view. Three people were entering the house: Barbara Anne, Faye, and Max. Somewhere he'd found his heart's desire, for Max now menaced them with a pistol.

"My sisters!" I told Charmaine.

"And if I'm not mistaken," Lars added, "my gun."

"What do we do now?" Charmaine asked.

The question didn't get answered, because Kylie stepped onto the porch, her own gun in hand. "Hey, Mr. FBI Agent, I'm guessing you're still close, so here's what's going to happen. These women stay alive as long as you let us leave without trouble. Anything slows us up, they die. Get it?" She listened to the stillness for a while, but of course we didn't answer. After a few seconds she called to Max, "Get the keys from these women. Find their car and bring it here."

"What for?"

"They probably called the cops already. Pull all the cars except Charmaine's behind the barn. If a cop shows up, he'll find one car and one old lady on the premises."

As Max went off to do as he was told, we huddled in the cold. My feet felt like Eskimo bars, and I pulled them under my legs.

"What's keeping them here?" Lars asked. "I've been stuck underground like a mole."

"Kylie's got a big deal cooking in Green Bay tomorrow."

Charmaine peered out the slats at the yard, where Max was busy moving cars. "I wouldn't count on finding your friends alive, no matter what Kylie promises."

Her tone was telling. "I take it you know the White family well?"

"Lydia and I were in the same grade in school. She moved away at eighteen, but when she came back she had those two grandkids." Her voice lowered. "Stealing is second nature to them."

"Somehow I'm not surprised," Lars said.

"They both left Green Bay for a while, but then Max came back and moved into the old family farmhouse. He stays there until it gets really cold; then I guess he sleeps at the store." She sniffed. "I didn't know they were still outlaws until they barged in here and stuck a gun in my face."

"Why'd they do that?"

She shivered, and I put an arm around her. "They needed a place to hide your truck, and they figured the police might check their place at some point. Knowing I'm alone, they barged in and took over."

199

"The deal they're waiting on must be something if they've hung around for this long," Lars said.

Charmaine shook her head, but I knew the answer to that one. "They have a piece of jewelry that's stunning, but apparently the buyer couldn't get here until now. They used the last few days to make it look like the sisters retired and moved to a warmer climate."

"People might believe it if they manage to kill all of us," Charmaine interjected.

"We have to get Faye and Barb out of there," Lars said.

"We aren't exactly safe ourselves, since we're likely to freeze to death out here." Charmaine shivered as she spoke, and Lars and I both put an arm around her, sharing our body heat.

"Look!" Lars said. A single sweep of headlights indicated that a car had entered the driveway. Soon the engine went silent, and there was a pause as I assumed the officer reported his arrival to dispatch. Then the car door opened and closed, and we heard the crunch of footsteps. When he moved into our slit of view, I saw a young deputy knocking on Charmaine's door. It opened, and there was DeeAnne, wearing an outfit I'd never have imagined: bib overalls, a flannel shirt, and muck boots. "Good evening, officer. What can I do for you?"

He seemed uncomfortable. "Are you the owner here, ma'am?"

Her head tilted to one side in a flirty manner and she said in her best Bette Davis voice, "Only for the last thirty years. Before that it belonged to my parents."

"I see. Well, we got a report there was some trouble out here."

She clutched at her chest. "Trouble? What do you mean?"

"There's people missing, and somebody said they might be here."

Her manner changed to relieved amusement. "Someone's having a joke on you, I'm afraid. There's no one here but me." After a pause she added, "You're welcome to come in and look."

"If you don't mind, ma'am. It will help if I can report that I checked the place out."

She swept the door fully open in a grand gesture. "I could make you a hot drink while you search. It's a cold night out there, and it would do you good."

I didn't hear his response, but I guessed he'd leave convinced things were just fine at the Dahlman place.

"Where would they hide them?"

"Attic, probably," Charmaine said. "The stairs pull up into the ceiling. Lydia visited as a kid, so she'd remember."

I imagined Max, Lydia, and Betty hunched in the cramped space, holding a gun on Barbara and Faye. I tried to picture them upright and glaring back at them. I didn't want to think about any other way things might play out.

Charmaine was still shivering violently. "Lars, she's going to freeze if we don't get her somewhere warm."

Lars stripped off his coat, insisting Charmaine put it on. After another long look at the house, he said, "I have an idea."

When he told us Charmaine asked, "What about you two?"

"If you do your part, we should all be okay."

"All right, but you have to take your coat back. If this works, I'll be warm soon enough." She took off the coat, and Lars said, "Can you get us out of here?"

"Sure thing." Crawling to the front, she once again stuck her fingers through the slats. I heard the hook spring free, and the door gaped. Charmaine turned to us, her face mostly black in the dark shed. "I'll get back with help as fast as I can."

"Great," Lars said, and she was gone.

"Now what?" I asked.

He pulled his coat on and stuck his hands into the pockets. "We wait, I guess."

After a moment I had another question. "Would it help if we waited somewhere warmer?"

"What do you mean?"

"They parked our vehicles behind the barn."

"Yes, but they took my keys. They must have taken yours too."

"They did, first thing. But I have kind of a habit of misplacing keys, so Barbara bought me one of those magnetic boxes you put in the wheel well."

Lars stood—or rather crouched, since there was no way he could stand in the tiny space. "Let's go get warm, Ms. Stilson. While we're de-icing, we can make a plan for getting your sisters out of that house."

CHAPTER FORTY-ONE

Barb

The attic wall was so slanted that I had to sit hunched over. I tried to ignore both my aching back and the negative side of my mind. "Some P.I. I am," I muttered. Faye shook her head to indicate I wasn't to blame.

"Quiet!" Lydia ordered. I obeyed, but the interior berating went on.

I'd been peering ahead, trying to get a glimpse of Faye, and Max had simply reached out from the shadows and twisted the gun from my hand. Yes, I'd been surprised. No, I hadn't expected him to be there. But twice I'd had firearms training, once as a young lawyer and once when I applied for an investigator's license. I'd been taught not to handle a gun carelessly. Now, like so many others who arm themselves thinking it will make them safer, I'd had my weapon turned against me. I vowed to do better in the future, but Ms. Negative in my head whispered I might not have much of a future.

Lydia and Kylie sat on either side of the single, tiny window in the attic. When they weren't craning their necks to look out, I had a clear view of the sheriff's car, parked half in shadow and half in the spill of light from above.

We sat in silence until Max joined us. "Got the last car up there just a few minutes before he showed up," he said softly. Lydia and Kylie nodded approval. Betty seemed to be napping—or was she catatonic?

Max was apparently unable to keep silent. "The fed and his woman are out there somewhere. What if they stop the deputy and tell him what's going on?"

"They believe we'd kill these two." Kylie said confidently. "When people know you won't hold back, they tend to do what you tell them to."

"Yeah," Max agreed. "Everybody knows you mean what you say."

Kylie turned to Lydia. "Once the cop leaves, you three can head for Minnesota in your car. Max will drop the truck off at the mill, walk to Lambeau, and I'll pick him up. We'll meet our guy at nine and sell him the necklace. By dinnertime we'll meet you in St. Paul."

"What if the police stop us on the road?" Lydia asked.

"We're not leaving by the route they'll expect," Kylie replied. "Max used Charmaine's tractor to plow the old cow-path that leads over to Collins Lane. We'll go out that way, and they'll never know we were here."

The door opened and closed downstairs, and Lydia said softly, "He's leaving."

They shrank away from the window, giving me a look at the scene below. The car's lights flashed as the deputy hit the unlock button. After opening the door, he turned to look back at the house for a moment. When he did, I thought I saw movement at the back of the car. It was hard to tell, since that side was away from me and fairly dark, but it looked like the back door opened and closed. The deputy got in and picked up his radio to report to the office. Had he gained a furtive passenger?

As soon as the engine started Kylie said, "Get things ready, Max. We need to be on our way."

Betty surprised us all, asking, "You're going to let these women go soon, right?"

"Of course, Aunt Betty. Now go with Max."

"Come on." Gently, Max guided Betty down the collapsible staircase. Lydia and Kylie followed, taking both flashlights with them. Faye and I sat in the dark, silent and out of hope.

Perhaps five minutes later, the ladder descended again and Betty's silver-topped head appeared in the opening. Below her stood a grumpy-looking Max, apparently there to assure we didn't overcome her and escape. A battery-operated lantern hung over Betty's arm, and she carried a tray with a plate of cookies and two cups of tea. Her smile was more suited to a luncheon with friends than provision of a last meal to condemned prisoners. Looking to Faye she said, "If you don't mind helping? My hip is tricky on these steps."

Faye rose, stepped forward, and took the tray from her. To our surprise, Betty sat down in the opening and folded her hands as if we were at a church picnic. "I'm sorry the cookies are store-bought," she said brightly. "It's all Charmaine had in the pantry." She spoke as if that were as great a sin as kidnapping.

"It's good of you to think of us," Faye said.

"I wanted to do something nice, since you fulfilled a lifelong dream of mine."

"Dream?" I asked.

Betty's face lit with happiness. "Didn't she tell you she brought my third-favorite person in the world to the store?" Realizing how that sounded, Betty backed up. "Outside of family, of course. Family always comes first."

"Your third-favorite person," I prompted.

"My first favorite is Bart Starr. Second is Brett Favre."

"Former Green Bay quarterbacks," I said for Faye's benefit.

"That's right!" Betty clasped her hands. "Did you see the game Brett played the day after he lost his father?"

I vaguely recalled it. "Didn't he pass for a lot of yards?"

"Three hundred and ninety-nine," she said. "Four touchdowns. Such a tribute to his daddy!"

"But Faye introduced you to your third-favorite person?"

"She did!" Betty put her fingers to her lips. "I couldn't believe it."

As I opened my mouth to ask who this wondrous person was, Max called out, "Come on, Aunt Betty. I got things to do."

"Go ahead, dear. I'll stay with these ladies until we're ready to set them free."

"I don't think Kye will like that," he warned.

Waving his concern away, she hobbled up the last few steps. "There. Close the hatch. Then they can't escape. I doubt either one of them will strangle me over tea and cookies." When Max looked doubtful she added, "Come back in ten minutes, Maxie. I'll be fine."

He left, muttering to himself, and Betty spoke candidly. "I'm just in the way down there." She adjusted the lantern so that it sat between us, lighting our faces and revealing the charm bracelet she wore, an assortment representing Green Bay's many championships. I noticed the hems of her slacks were bordered with appliquéd footballs. "Lydia and Kye run things now."

"But the business was yours to start with."

"I was just barely paying my expenses." She waved a hand. "Strictly small-time, Lydia says."

"But honest."

"Can't make money being honest." That sounded like another quote from Lydia, and Betty's gaze dropped. "It was my fault your sister and her friend had to be locked up."

"Because they saw the stolen stuff."

If Betty suspected we were to be killed, would she do something about it? The next question was *could* she do anything about it. Betty was naïve. She was outnumbered. And she was a little cuckoo. Right now she was all we had.

Moving close to Faye so I could set a hand on her back I said, "Yes, my sister sure loves the Packers."

I felt Faye's back tense, but I squeezed, signaling her to play along. "Always," she echoed, though her voice was faint.

"Which do you think was better this year," Betty asked, "our O-line or the D?"

I drew a *D* on Faye's back, emphasizing the straight line. "Definitely D."

"I agree. We need to draft some receivers to make the offense work." Clearly pleased, she asked, "What's your favorite Super Bowl win?" I searched my mind for a year. "We liked the '68 win best, wouldn't you say, Faye?"

Faye answered a little too quickly. "Yes. That one."

"Of course it wasn't called the Super Bowl then, but yes, Bart Starr was amazing. Got his second MVP."

"Amazing," Faye said.

"His passing was great." I didn't really know that, but it was a decent guess that a winning quarterback would pass well. "Especially with how cold it was."

Betty frowned. "Super Bowl II was played in Miami."

"Of course." I tapped Faye's shoulder with my free hand. "She remembers stuff like that better than I do, right, Faye?"

"Right." Her smile was weak as water.

"You're thinking of the Ice Bowl," Betty said, "the last playoff game that year. We beat the Cowboys in a wind chill of minus forty degrees on the field." Betty's false teeth loomed at us in the dimness as she added, "I was there."

"Wow," Faye said. "I hope you were dressed for it."

"It's Green Bay." Her tone hinted the response might have been "*Duh!*"

I gave Faye a little shake to indicate that weather concerns weren't what Betty wanted to discuss. She tossed me a sideways glance that said she was doing the best she could.

"How often do you come to see a game?" Betty asked.

I pressed on Faye's back twice and she said, "We try to come a couple times each season." Inspired by our recent experience she added, "The traffic's become a problem though."

"I've seen that, though I usually walk from our place. No parking fees, no traffic jams."

"You're really lucky."

Betty's eyes glowed with pleasure. "I am. Some things in life don't work out, you know, but there are always things that do. I have my cats and my team. That's enough."

"It's too bad you have to leave Green Bay."

"True." She looked regretful. "But Lydia says we'll be able to travel with the team. I'll be a little sad not to be able to go to Lambeau for games, but I'll still see the boys play."

Faye moved uncomfortably. Betty White had never had a husband or children of her own to love. The business she'd devoted decades to had been taken over by others and turned into something she only vaguely recognized. At eighty years of age, Betty had only cats and the Pack to love. Big-hearted Faye was feeling sorry for her.

I was trying to decide how we could use her to get out of that attic.

"What will happen to your cats when you give up the store?"

Betty blinked as if the change of topic was hard for her. "They'll ride in the truck with Maxie."

"Does he have enough carriers for all of them?"

"Not yet, but he said he'll take care of it soon."

"That's good. You're already leaving your football team behind. You wouldn't want to leave your cats too."

She looked horrified. "We'd never do that."

"Will they all fit in the cab? They shouldn't have to ride in the back, where it's cold."

More blinks. "I'm not sure. Maxie just said he'd handle it."

I spoke softly. "Betty, are you sure they're telling you the truth?"

"Of course they are, dear." She touched the Green Bay Packers watch on her wrist. "Family doesn't lie to family."

CHAPTER FORTY-TWO

Retta

Leaving the corn crib, Lars and I made our way up the hill in the shadows. The wind had come up, and it hummed through the trees at our side. Behind Charmaine's barn we found five vehicles: my SUV, Lars' pickup, the Critterz flatbed, a van I guessed was Kylie's, and a PT Cruiser loaded with suitcases. They were lined up like Tonka toys, and I slipped between the pickup and my car, sliding a hand along the fender until I found the small metal case stuck to the underside. In seconds we were inside, with the engine running and the heater turned on full blast.

For a while I just sat there and shivered, but then I realized that the back of the car was literally stuffed with my things. Crawling over the seat, I located shoes, dry socks, a sweater to put on under my coat, and a spare pair of gloves. Climbing back to the front I told Lars, "Much better. Now tell me about Charmaine and how you two met."

"Charmaine is the second-most charming woman I've ever been imprisoned with," Lars replied, holding his hands close to the blower. "Max and Kylie took over her home and locked her in her pantry. They didn't realize there was a window behind one of the shelving units. Charmaine took all her canned goods off the shelves, wrestled the unit away from the wall, and climbed out. She'd planned to use her four-wheeler to get away, but Max had taken the key with him. Hoping to push-start it, she put the thing in neutral and guided it off the cellar doors." He chuckled. "She was pretty surprised when I popped up."

"How long do you think it will be before the police get here?"

"I'm hoping no more than twenty minutes. It kind of depends on where the sheriff's cars are when the call goes out." He shrugged, and I knew what he meant. If they were on the other side of the county, it might be forty minutes. "As soon as we're warmed up, we'll go through the trees and meet them on the road."

"Where do you think they've got Faye and Barbara?"

"I'm thinking Charmaine's right. The attic." After a moment he added, "We can't get to them without that bunch knowing about it."

"Lars, they plan to blow up the house before they go."

He made an anguished groan. "Then we can't wait for the police."

A sound I'd been hearing finally broke through my consciousness. Rolling down the window, I listened for a moment.

A bark. A dog's bark. *My* dog's bark.

"Lars! Styx is here somewhere."

"What?"

"Faye must have brought him along."

"But where is he?" Lars asked. "If Max had seen him he'd have..." He paused, unwilling to add to my worry.

"Wherever he is, he's well enough to bark." I opened the door, but Lars grabbed my arm.

"I'll go. Do you have a flashlight?"

"Of course." I dug it out and handed it to him. "Be careful."

It didn't take long, but I was a wreck the whole time. Despite the cold and the wind, I rolled the window down and listened. Yes, it was Styx, his bark muted but constant. When it stopped, I thought my heart might do the same thing.

212

Had something bad happened? Focusing on the spot where I'd last seen Lars, I strained against the dark. At first nothing moved, but then I saw a flash of white—the front of Lars' shirt showing under his coat. He hurried toward me with the biggest bundle ever in his arms. I gasped when I saw a dark stain on Lars' shirt. Blood.

Getting out, I opened the hatch so he could lay Styx inside. "Styx! Oh, my poor baby!"

Styx whined once, and his usually buoyant personality was gone. "Where was he?"

"Locked in with some cows." Lars examined to locate the source of bleeding. On his hip was a puncture wound.

"Is he badly hurt?" Remembering I had a first aid kit, I hurried to the front and got it.

Lars took the plastic box from me. "The wound is pretty small and not very deep, like he fell on something metal."

"A pitchfork." I felt responsible, though that was uncalled-for. How could I have known Styx would fall onto the tool I'd tossed aside?

"I'll do the best I can for right now." He took some salve from the kit and smeared it on the wound. Then he stuck a large gauze pad over it. "I hope he'll leave that on, but no guarantees."

"Poor baby!"

"That's all we can do for him right now, Retta. We have to get to Faye and Barb."

I agreed, though I felt like I was being torn in two. "Rest, baby," I told Styx. "We'll be back soon."

When Lars closed the hatch, Styx didn't even whimper. It was like he knew we wouldn't leave him if it weren't absolutely necessary. It felt like betrayal, but with my sisters' lives at stake, what choice did I have?

CHAPTER FORTY-THREE

Barb

"Betty!" Lydia's voice came from below. "Get down here. We're leaving!" The folding stairs creaked down to the floor, and her head appeared in the opening.

With a glance at us Betty said, "Then we can let these ladies get back to their car, right?"

"Max will see to that. We need to go now."

"It's been really nice meeting you." Betty spoke mostly to Faye.

Faye seemed at a loss, as was I. It would do no good to tell Betty we were going to die as soon as she left the property. She wouldn't believe it. She wouldn't accept it. And to be honest, she couldn't actually do anything about it.

We sat in the dark for a few seconds before I realized that something was different. "Faye, look."

Light showed around the pull-down stairs—not much, since the floor below us was unlit. Crawling to the opening, I pressed tentatively on the folded ladder. "It's not latched."

Faye joined me. "She was in a hurry and didn't close it all the way."

"Or Betty isn't as unaware as they think she is."

Pushing the ladder downward, I waited to see if anyone would stop me. No one did. It tapped softly on the wood floor below, and no one came to see what the noise was. Silently, slowly, we descended to the second story. With more and larger windows there was more light. I saw that Faye's hair was coated with spider web, and she had streaks of dust across the rear of her pants. No doubt I looked the same.

The staircase to the main floor took a ninety-degree turn halfway down. With no idea what we'd find, we tiptoed down to the landing and stopped. We could see no one. I heard voices: Betty, Lydia, and Kylie.

"Are you sure you meant what you said?" Betty asked. "You're really going to let them go?"

"Of course, Aunt Betty," Kylie replied, though the edge in her voice was evident.

"Then why is Maxie going to blow up the house?"

There was a pause, and I imagined Kylie looking to Lydia for help. "Fingerprints, Betty. We can't let the police know we were here. Now get your overnight bag and put it in DeeAnne's car."

"All right." Betty was so trusting it made me want to scream. I heard her uneven steps as she did as she was told. When she was out of hearing Kylie said, "Gram, I can't deal with her anymore."

"What do you mean?"

A sigh. "It's her fault that fed saw our stuff. She was always dumb, but now she's drifty too. What will we do with her in a new place? She's liable to tell people we used to be thieves but we retired."

"She wouldn't."

"Really, Gram? Really?"

Lydia's voice went flat. "What do you propose?"

"She stays here with her new friends. They all go together."

Lydia's voice got tight. "DeeAnne would never agree to that. Or Max either."

"They don't need to know how it happens. Maybe one of those women pushed her down the attic stairs."

"You want me to let you murder my sister?"

"In six months she won't even know you're her sister." Kylie's voice was cold. "Every day she's less attached to reality. Ten times a day she does something that puts us in danger. DeeAnne can't handle her anymore, and you and I have better things to do than babysit." She sniffed. "Do what you want, but if Betty comes along, I'm taking my share and getting out. I am not going to prison because of her."

"I—I—just can't—"

When Lydia couldn't finish, Kylie's voice took on a commanding tone. "You don't have to do anything. Just take DeeAnne and leave. Tell her Betty's with Max, and I'll tell Max she left with you."

I never heard Lydia's answer, never knew if she said anything at all. Faye and I had to lean back as someone passed the staircase. I peeped out to see Max's skinny back disappear into the kitchen. As we waited silently on the dark stairs, Kylie told him, "We're just about ready to leave. You can bring our guests downstairs."

Glancing at Faye I mouthed, "Noise!" Understanding immediately, she retreated while I flattened myself along the wall. As Max started up the stairs, I realized my best chance was to do to him exactly what he'd done to me.

When Max stepped onto the landing, Faye began stomping her feet, making it sound like a herd of racing camels was up there. Starting in surprise, Max stuck his gun hand out at arm's length, the classic—and generally wrong—way people do in movies. Reaching out, I grabbed the barrel and gave it a vicious sideways twist. Max roared in anger and pain, but the gun was mine. Reacting quickly, he turned and retreated.

Faye and I followed, but we were a lot slower than Max. I heard him shout, "Kye! They're loose!" Then the outside door slammed. He wasn't about to stick around and face getting shot.

Lying on the counter were the phones he'd taken from us, turned off to prevent tracking. I handed Faye hers. "Go out the front door and head for the road," I told her. "Call the police, the fire department, everyone you can think of."

She opened her mouth to object, but I said, "Go! If one of us gets away, killing the others won't be worthwhile to them."

A hand on my arm said a lot of things: *Be careful. I love you. I hope we both live through this.* Then she was gone.

CHAPTER FORTY-FOUR

Faye

I made my way to the front of the house, where a largely unused door led outside from what had once been a parlor, but was now an office of sorts. A computer desk took up one whole corner, and the old furniture, a settee, a couple of chairs, and some carved end tables, had been shoved together to make room for modern times. The door faced the road, but there was no path. I'd have to wade through knee-deep snow. At least the front of the house was dark, so I'd have cover.

Passing the computer table, I noticed a box lying open. In it was a velvet bag, and just visible at the neck of the bag was something shiny. I paused long enough to draw the bag back. A necklace. While I'm no jewelry expert, I guessed it was valuable, probably the reason for the skullduggery of the last few days.

Sweeping up the box, I headed on to the front door. It presented a few problems, like a sticky handle and a grating sill, but I managed to wrench it open and step into the night.

Taking a moment to look and listen, I tried to read the situation. On the hilltop behind the barn, a PT Cruiser appeared briefly then disappeared into the woods, apparently taking a road I hadn't noticed earlier. One of more of the White sisters were on their way to Minnesota. I heard a small engine start up somewhere behind me and turned. Was it the 4-wheeler I'd seen beside the house? It ran for only a few seconds then cut out abruptly. Peering around the corner of the house, I saw Kylie standing near the door, gun in hand. I wanted to warn Barb, but of course she knew the danger she was in. Going back inside would only confuse the situation. I had my phone, and my job was to call for help.

Looking around for a place of safety, I saw a picket fence, once decorative, now mostly an eyesore. It offered a hiding place, so I waded to it, climbed over, and squatted in the trough of a snowdrift on the opposite side.

As I pulled up my contacts, another idea came to me. When we believed Kylie was Agent Stiles, Barb had programmed her number into my phone as well as her own. I could call and make a deal.

The phone rang and rang, but finally an impatient voice said, "What do you want?" It was Lydia, not Kylie. What had she decided to do with Betty? Had she sent DeeAnne off alone? How many did we still have to deal with?

"I want you to stop trying to kill us, for one thing."

"Because you're asking so nicely?"

"No. Because I have the necklace."

I heard a muttered expletive. "Give it back!"

"When you release Retta and everyone else you're holding captive, I'll do exactly that."

There was a long pause. "Let me see what I can do." The call ended.

What did that mean?

I didn't have long to wonder, because the phone vibrated only a minute later. "Hello?"

"Faye," Dale's sister said, "I know it's early, but you're up at the butt-crack of dawn, so I didn't think you'd mind me calling." I figured that meant with the time difference that it was somewhere around five a.m. in Michigan, four in Wisconsin. "I just want to say a couple of things. You know and I know that Mom never took to you, and she said some really mean things behind your back. I always defended you, and I was glad you and Dale managed to stay together." I might have laughed at that, had my situation been less dire. "But that's why you should get what you deserve from her money. She owes you. Now I talked to that lawyer again, and she says—"

I held the phone away from my face, unable to comprehend what was happening. My sisters were in danger of being blown to smithereens. We struggled against thieves-turned-murderers in the dark of—what? Night? Early morning? I huddled in a snowbank, shivering with cold. I wasn't sure help would arrive in time to save us.

And for the first time in thirty-five years, my sister-in-law wanted to make nice.

"Wanda," I said quietly but forcefully. "Listen carefully. Do not call me again, ever. You—you are—consistently and unceasingly annoying!"

I stabbed the *End* button and went back to waiting. The next time the phone buzzed, I checked the caller ID before answering. "I'm listening."

It was Kylie. "Bring the box to the door. I'll leave; you'll go in. As we pass, you hand me the box. I leave, and you get your people, all safe and sound."

"That doesn't work for me. In the first place, I don't know that they're even alive."

"They're locked in the storeroom off the kitchen," she informed me. "They're fine."

"Why would I trust you on that?"

"How do I know you're not going to bring me an empty box?"

221

"How do I know you won't just shoot me if I show up? Or blow up the house as you walk away?"

Her hesitation indicated that one or both of those things had been on her mind. "We have to make this work," she finally said in a sulky tone. "What do you propose?"

"I'll set the necklace in a place where you can see it from a distance. You bring Retta, Mrs. Dahlin, and Lars out so I can see they're okay."

She snorted a laugh. "I can't watch three of them and both of you at the same time." That meant she didn't know Barb was still in the house. Good.

"All right. Just bring Retta. I'll take her word for it that Lars and Mrs. Dahlin are safe."

It was a gamble, but Kylie had to know by now the police were on their way. She could no longer hide her crimes by killing her captives, so her best bet was to do exactly as I said, get the necklace in exchange for her prisoners, and leave before they arrived. "Okay. Give me a minute and I'll meet you at the door."

Hoping to give myself an advantage, I threw her a little curve. "Make it the front door," I said. "And turn on the porch light so I can see you." The door was outside the yard light's spill, she wouldn't be able to see me, which meant she couldn't shoot me. That was my hope; I had to play the odds.

While I waited for her, I called the Brown County Sheriff's Department. I was informed that cars were on the way and I should "shelter in place." I told them about the old cow path that led to a different road, and they'd promised to cover that exit too. Unable to guess when the police would arrive, I decided to give Kylie the necklace and let her go. Once everyone was safe, they could catch up with her on the road.

CHAPTER FORTY-FIVE

Retta

Our plan made, Lars and I left the shelter of the car. Lars rounded the barn to the right and crept from shadow to shadow toward the house, intending to find my sisters. I went around the barn in the other direction, heading toward the road so I could update the police when they arrived. As I reached the edge of the woods, I heard gunshots. Turning, I saw Max bolt from the house like his shirt-tail was on fire. First he went to the flatbed and rattled around in the cab for a few seconds. He exited looking frustrated, and I concluded the keys were in the house somewhere. Looking around the yard, he stopped when his gaze hit the four-wheeler. If he was in search of a getaway vehicle, and I figured he was, off-road was a perfect choice for avoiding the police.

Max glanced up at the barn, and I leaned into the trees to avoid notice. The track that led up the hill continued into the woods, perhaps to a secondary exit.

If that was his plan, he had to come directly past me.

Max's haste worked in my favor. He beat frantically at his pockets, trying to find which one he'd put the key in. By the time he found it, I had a weapon in hand: a fist-sized tree branch. Max got on the four-wheeler and pressed the starter. The engine was sluggish due to the cold, which gave me time to sprint to the far corner of the barn and disappear behind it. When the four-wheeler finally started, I could no longer see it, so I had to gauge Max's progress by sound. He wrenched it into gear, turned it around, and headed up the hill toward me. Judging the right moment was difficult, but I heard the change in pitch when the machine started uphill. It bogged a little as it fought icy patches and frozen trenches in the track. Max had to concentrate on his driving, so he didn't see me step out just before he rounded the corner. He'd just begun to build up speed, and the branch braced against my shoulder like a jouster's lance hit him in his ratty little face.

I was spun in a circle by the force of the blow, and the branch disintegrated into kindling. The ATV went on for a little way then hit a snowdrift and stalled. When I recovered my balance, I was gratified to see Max flat on the ground, his nose bloody and his eyes blank. While he was still mumbling, "What happened?" I dragged him through the barn doorway. "Let's see if you've got any more of those zip-ties in your pockets."

He had two. Perfect. As I bound his hands and feet I advised, "I'll send the cops to get you in a little while. Make yourself a nest in the hay, and you'll stay warm."

CHAPTER FORTY-SIX

Barb

I went in the opposite direction Faye took, intending to exit through the kitchen. Something whizzed past my head, and with a jolt of fear, I realized Kylie was shooting at me. Without stopping to aim, I fired a couple of shots in her general direction, just to make her cautious. I continued to the door in a crouch, pulled it open, and threw myself through. I breathed the cold air in deeply. Freedom!

Or not. As I hurried down the steps, I bumped into something substantial that knocked me back on my heels. A big hand reached out and grabbed my coat, and a towering figure pulled me close. When I looked up, I laughed aloud. Lars.

Though as surprised as I to see a friendly face, he recovered quickly. Pulling me to a spot out of the security light's reach he asked, "Where's Faye?"

"I sent her out front to meet the police. Where's Retta?"

"Doing the same thing. Charmaine Dahlman escaped in the back of the deputy's car."

That was a relief. Much of the White family's incentive to kill us disappeared if the place was surrounded by flashing lights and uniformed officers. If Retta and Faye were safe, and the owner of the house too, all Lars and I had to do was get to safety and let the police handle the situation.

"We need to go." Lars tugged at my arm. "Retta says they've rigged the house to explode."

I stopped short. "Lars, Kylie planned to leave Betty behind. We have to get her out of there."

An outrush of breath told me he was as unhappy about that as I was. "Go out back, find the gas pig, and turn off the main valve. There's a cover you lift. The shutoff will be inside.

"Here," I whispered, handing him his gun. The change in his demeanor was immediate, and he checked the ammunition. "I suppose it's too much to ask for the spare clip."

"I figured they'd search us, so I moved it to...here." Reaching into my bra, I pulled the clip out and handed it to him.

Even in our dire situation, Lars grinned. "Good thinking." His face sobered. "Once you turn off the gas, get out of here."

"Where will you be?"

"If you shut everything down, that should take care of the problem, but just in case, I'll find Betty and get her out."

"Got it." Lars was putting his life in my hands, and it wasn't just the cold that made me shiver.

He left me then, hurrying up the steps and leaning to the side as he turned the knob. When no gunfire erupted, he slid inside and closed the door softly.

The gas pig sat at the back of the house, a cylindrical tube the size of a rowboat. On top was a housing for the shut-off. I slogged my way to it through the snow, climbed the metal frame, and tilted the cover back. It was fairly easy to turn the valve, and I felt a great sense of accomplishment. For a few seconds.

Questions poured into my mind. When had Max opened the gas pipe? Had enough gas leaked out to cause an explosion? I had to get fresh air from the outside to replace the poison spreading inside.

It took a few seconds to find the means, but someone had tossed a pry-bar onto the ground near the first window I came to. Picking it up, I smashed the glass with a single blow then went on to the next. The kitchen window was higher than the rest, but a metal garbage can stood nearby. It was difficult to move, being half full, but I walked it over to the window, climbed atop it, and smashed the glass.

Though there was no one in the kitchen, the microwave was running. Recalling a novel I'd read where an aerosol can heated in a microwave had ignited an explosion, I reached in with the crowbar and pulled the plug.

That was when the shooting started again. I jumped to the ground, feet sliding in my haste to get out of the way. After a few rounds, four, maybe five, I heard a scream and a curse. Kylie. Next I heard Lars' voice, commanding and sure. "Put your hands up and come out."

"I'm shot!" she cried. "You shot me, you—"

"Slide the gun out into the hallway," he told her. "Put your hands where I can see them. Once you do that, I'll call in the EMTs." After a pause he added, "If you don't want to go that route, I'll just wait until you pass out from loss of blood. Either way works for me."

CHAPTER FORTY-SEVEN

Faye

There was a lot going on at the back of the house, but I couldn't see it from my hiding place. Gunshots, glass breaking, and shouts of alarm made me quiver with dread, but I felt fairly safe huddled behind the old picket fence like a rabbit in its burrow. When the porch light came on and the door opened, I peered between the pickets, fearful Kylie might come out shooting.

Lydia Peete appeared in the doorway, steering her sister Betty in front of her like a human shield. She held a gun at Betty's waist, and while I doubted Betty understood what was happening, it was clear she was the hostage in this scenario.

"Are you here?" she called out.

"Yes." I kept it brief, hoping she couldn't locate me by one short utterance.

"Give the box to Betty and let us pass. If you do anything to slow me down, I will shoot." Though she didn't specify, Lydia indicated with the gun barrel that her sister was the target. While she couldn't locate me, she couldn't miss Betty. It was a gamble in which she counted on my reluctance to see Betty get hurt. I couldn't tell if Betty understood what was happening, but her posture seemed more stooped than usual, as if something weighed heavily on her shoulders.

"Is that my Packer friend?" she asked tremulously.

"It is," Lydia answered. "She's going to give you a box that you and I will take with us to Arizona. DeeAnne is already on her way, so we need to hurry to catch up with her. Can you carry the box for me?"

"Of course I can, Lydia." Betty sounded almost snappish. "I'm not helpless."

"Of course you aren't." Lydia raised her voice, ordering, "Come out and hand Betty the box."

I did as I was told, unable to think of an alternative. Taking it, she showed Lydia that the necklace was inside. When she nodded Betty said to me, "Thanks so much, dear. I'm sorry we've kept you from your sister all this time. Family is so important." Looking toward the driveway, she frowned. "I only see Charmaine's car. Is that what we're taking?"

"Only as far as the barn. I have the keys to Ms. Starkey's SUV."

It took me a second to figure that one out. "You mean Stilson."

Lydia made an impatient gesture. "Whatever. Let's go, Betty." She held the gun on me while Betty got into the old sedan.

I couldn't resist asking, "Would you really have shot your own sister for a piece of jewelry?

She looked thoughtful. "I'm not sure, but I certainly would have shot you if necessary."

She got into the car, started it up, and drove up the incline.

I gave them about thirty seconds before I followed.

CHAPTER FORTY-EIGHT

Barb

I reached Balsam Road to find several police cars, a dark, unmarked sedan, and a dozen people huddled in the cold: eight sheriff's department officers, some others I later learned were tribal police, a man in a suit, and a woman who spoke as they all listened intently.

"They were all in the house when I left," she was saying, "but they plan to blow it up, so don't go running in there."

Someone heard me coming, and suddenly I had twelve suspicious faces and a couple of firearms turned in my direction.

"I was a hostage," I told them. "My sister and I escaped, but I don't know where our other sister is."

Behind me a motor started up, throttled to full, roared for maybe thirty seconds, and then died. "What was that?" the man in the suit asked.

"Four-wheeler," the woman said. "Whoever took it didn't get far. We escaped too," the woman told me. "I'm Charmaine Dahlman, and Lars sent me to get help." It was a relief to know that Lars and Retta were still among the living. She went on with the introductions. "This is Sheriff Talkert, and that gentleman is Agent Jamie Stiles of the FBI." She waved at the others. "Now what are we going to do about saving my house?"

"I hope I solved the problem," I told her. "I shut off the gas and— I'm afraid I broke a bunch of windows."

She waved that away. "That's what I have insurance for."

A sheriff's car pulled up beside us, and a young deputy got out. "I'm not sure I did the right thing, sir," he began. "You sent out a call to stop and detain a PT Cruiser, but...she's an old lady!"

Charmaine peered into the car. "DeeAnne," she said with obvious satisfaction.

The kid frowned. "She's really a criminal then? Because she told me all about how she's in a hurry to get to Minnesota because her granddaughter needs a bone-marrow transplant, and she's a match that will save the kid's life."

"She lied," Charmaine said flatly. "I've known Miss DeeAnne for almost seventy years, and she's really good at it."

CHAPTER FORTY-NINE

Retta

I'd just finished hog-tying Max when I heard a car approaching. As I peeped out, Charmaine's Chevy passed the loft door. Lydia was driving, and I thought Betty sat in the passenger seat. The car went around the back of the barn and stopped, and I listened as Lydia spoke to her sister.

"Get in the SUV, Betty."

"But it's not ours. Ms. Stilson's going to need it to get home."

Lydia's tone hardened. "Get in, Betty." In a lower voice she muttered, "Maybe Kylie was right about this."

Betty had apparently reached her limit. "I don't think I want to go to Arizona. I'll just stay at the mill. Maybe I'll come and visit you sometimes, but Green Bay is my home."

"Betty." She spoke through her teeth. "If you stay, they'll put you in prison."

Her answer rang with disbelief. "I'll tell the police what happened, and they'll understand." Her tone changed abruptly. "Lydia, you aren't supposed to point a weapon at anyone."

"Get in the SUV."

I heard the door locks disengage at the same moment I sensed movement beside me. Faye put her finger to her lips, and I managed to remain quiet, though I hugged her fiercely.

"Get in, Betty," Lydia repeated. "We're going *now*, or I swear I'll shoot you and leave you behind."

One of them opened a car door, and that's when things got wild. Styx roared to life, letting out a bark that scared even me, and I'm used to him. Betty screamed. Lydia swore. Faye took off, and I followed. As we came around the corner, we separated. Faye went for Betty, pulling her to a crouch behind the car so her sister couldn't shoot her. I headed for Lydia, who was actually not that much of a threat anymore. Styx stood on top of her, and the gun lay ten feet away. Though she struggled to get out from under the dog, he was more than a match for her, even with a damaged hip. I picked the gun up and said, "Okay, Styx. I've got this. Lydia, stay right where you are or so help me—"

A voice behind me said, "We'll take over now ma'am. Don't go bopping her on the head before the judge gets a chance to put her in jail." I turned to see two officers standing behind me. I hadn't even noticed when they turned their super-bright flashlights on us.

Standing up from behind the car Betty said cheerfully, "You didn't tell me you had a pet, Retta. I love kitties, but I like doggies too."

CHAPTER FIFTY

Faye

Charmaine Dahlman gave each of us a big hug. "Thanks for saving the old place," she muttered gruffly. "It isn't much, but it's what I've got."

"Thanks for getting the deputy to call in the cavalry," Lars replied.

"You know what?" Charmaine asked. "Sheriff thinks Betty sabotaged things."

"Betty?"

"Yes. Max claims he'd have been gone, but the truck keys were missing. Sheriff found them in Betty's pocket."

Recalling the unlatched attic door, I wondered aloud, "Was that deliberate?"

"She's not saying. She just asks when she can see her cats again."

I shook my head. "Poor thing. I don't suppose they'll let her have a cat in prison."

Lars shook his head. "More likely she'll be sent to a secure dementia unit."

"That would be fair." Barb returned to the group, having called Rory to report that we were all safe. "I think she finally realized they were stringing her along when they lied about bringing her cats."

"There's a sweetness to Betty the other two never had," Charmaine said. "DeeAnne was always in love with herself, and Lydia is just plain mean."

It took a few phone calls, but we managed to communicate to everyone who needed to know that the situation was resolved and we were okay. Retta and Lars left to find a "V-E-T" for Styx. (She spelled it so he didn't hear the word and get anxious.) He didn't seem badly hurt, but cleaning a puncture wound is always important to prevent tetanus, rare in dogs but still possible. Styx was so glad to have Retta back he'd have gone anywhere with her.

Barb spoke at length to Rory, her voice softer than usual. I heard her promise to come home as soon as possible. He said something, and she laughed like Barb seldom does, low in her throat and happy.

I called Dale and told him the story, glossing over the more dangerous parts so he wouldn't fuss. When we'd talked that out I told him, with some reluctance, about Wanda's many calls. I was sick about it, sure I'd caused trouble for Dale and discord in the family.

"Don't worry about Wanda," Dale told me. "In the first place, she won't stay mad for long. She fights with everybody, so if she held grudges, she'd soon run out of people to talk to."

"I guess that's true," I said doubtfully, "but I've spent all these years trying not to cause a family fight, and—I kind of told her off."

"With good reason," he replied. "Wanda started with me, telling how ma was out of her head and 'we' should take another look at the will. I told her no first thing." He paused, and I pictured him rubbing his neck. "I suppose she thought you could talk me into it, since I care more about what you think than I do the whole bunch of them."

That made me feel better. "I can't wait to get home and give you a great big hug, Mr. Burner."

"I'll be right here, Mrs. Burner. And your dog will too, though he'll probably snub you for a while as punishment for leaving him behind."

That afternoon we again said goodbye to Retta and Lars. "Try to stay out of trouble this time," Barb joked.

"And you drive safely going home," Retta ordered. Glancing at Lars, who was busy loading their vehicles, she confided, "I think this move might be temporary, so you aren't rid of me just yet."

"What do you mean?"

"Lars got a job offer."

I was confused. "He already has a job."

"True, but he can retire at fifty with twenty years of service, which he'll reach in a few months." She checked again. Lars was cleaning the back window of her car. The outside had a salt film and the inside had patches of dried dog drool. "A few years back," she told us, "Lars worked with a certain notable American. This person has asked him to spend a year abroad with him as his personal security adviser."

"Which notable American are we talking about?"

"That's a secret until he decides whether to take the job, but I'll just say he's one of Barbara Ann's favorite political figures ever." Retta glanced at Lars, who went into the office, presumably to take leave of Mr. Hauer. We'd managed to find a hotel room for Barb and me, which was a relief, but Retta, Lars, and Styx had remained at the Pack-Rack, for sentimental reasons, I suppose.

"If he takes the job, he'll be leaving the U.S. in April, so I'll come back home and wait for him there," Retta said. "If he decides to stay with the Bureau, we'll stay in Albuquerque until he retires, which he says won't be more than two years."

"Retiring is a big decision," Barb said. "And fifty is pretty young."

"But you did it and then found something else to work at," Retta responded. "Lars is a planner. He'd thought it all through, but then this job offer came along. It's a really good opportunity for him."

Barb asked what responsibilities Lars would take on if he went overseas, and she seemed impressed with Retta's answers. I thought Retta was happy for Lars and content with whichever path he chose. And me? I was pleased with the prospect that either way, Retta would be coming home soon, and all three of us would be in Allport, where we belong.

ABOUT THE AUTHOR

Maggie Pill is also Peg Herring, but Maggie's much younger and cooler.

Visit http://maggiepill.maggiepillmysteries.com

or http://pegherring.com for more great mysteries.

Have you read Book #1, *The Sleuth Sisters*, yet?

Learn how the sisters started their detective agency, found a long-lost murder suspect, and almost went from three sisters to two.

How about Book #2, *3 Sleuths, 2 Dogs, 1 Murder*?

When Retta's "gentleman friend" is arrested for murder, the sisters brave a winter wilderness, far from rescue. Three determined women, with help from two dogs and a pair of horses, can do anything. Sister Power!

Book #3, **Murder in the Boonies**

Renters on the family farm disappear without a trace, and the sisters are left to solve the mystery, deal with a menagerie, and stop a plot that would spell disaster for Michigan's famous Mackinac Island.

Book #4, **Sleuthing at Sweet Springs**

Visiting a nursing home, Faye meets a woman who claims she doesn't belong there. Trying to help leads the sisters into big trouble, and—who'd have guessed—a flock of helpful chickens!

Book #5, **Eat, Drink, and Be Wary**

Retta and Faye take on a case Barb won't touch, a gathering of "girly" women. When murder strikes and her sisters are in trouble, she's there, of course, but it turns out to be dangerous for all of them.

Book #6, **Peril, Plots, and Puppies**

When Barb and Retta bust a puppy mill, Faye takes a personal interest in finding homes for every dog. At the same time, Barb is almost caught on one of her Correction Events because of a murder nearby.

Books available from Amazon in print, e-book, & audiobook, and most other e-book providers (B&N, Kobo, etc.). Also at Ingram for bookstore orders.

Books by Peg Herring

The Simon & Elizabeth Mysteries *(Tudor Era Historical)*

Her Highness' First Murder
Poison, Your Grace
The Lady Flirts with Death
Her Majesty's Mischief
***

The Loser Mysteries *(Contemporary Mystery/Suspense)*

Killing Silence
Killing Memories
Killing Despair
***

Clan Macbeth Historical Romance (medieval Scotland)

Macbeth's Niece
Double Toil & Trouble
***

Standalone Mysteries

Somebody Doesn't Like Sarah Leigh (contemporary cozy mystery)
Her Ex-GI P.I. ('60s-era mystery)
Not Dead Yet... ('60s-era paranormal mystery)
Shakespeare's Blood (thriller)

Kidnap Capers (Thrillers with cozy tendencies)

KIDNAP.org (Book 1)
Pharma Con (Book 2)